P9-CLI-510

A Higher Geometry

A Higher Geometry

SHARELLE BYARS MORANVILLE

HENRY HOLT AND COMPANY

NEW YORK

Henry Holt and Company, LLC
Publishers since 1866
175 Fifth Avenue
New York, New York 10010
www.henryholtchildrensbooks.com

Library of Congress Cataloging-in-Publication Data
Moranville, Sharelle Byars.
A higher geometry / Sharelle Byars Moranville.—1st ed.
p.   cm.
Summary: While grieving the death of her grandmother in 1959,
teenager Anna is torn between her aspirations to study math in college
and her family's expectations that she will marry and become a home-
maker after high school.
ISBN-13: 978-0-8050-7470-3 / ISBN-10: 0-8050-7470-8
[1. Sex role—Fiction.   2. Mathematics—Fiction.   3. Grief—Fiction.
4. High schools—Fiction.   5. Schools—Fiction.   6. United States—
History—1953–1961—Fiction.]   I. Title.
PZ7.M78825Hig 2006   [Fic]—dc22   2005021699

Illustrations and book design by Laurent Linn
First edition—2006
Printed in the United States of America on acid-free paper. ∞

1   3   5   7   9   10   8   6   4   2

To my husband, Barry;
my nephew, David;
and my editor, Christy

Acknowledgment

I'm very grateful to my nephew, David Jackson, for his conception of the Chicago scene—as well as for his enthusiastic and tireless discussion of mathematics during the writing of the manuscript.

A Higher Geometry

Part 1: Fall

Mathematicians are like lovers. Grant a mathematician the least principle, and he will draw from it a consequence which you must also grant him, and from this consequence another.

—BERNARD LE BOVIER DE FONTENELLE (1657–1757), FRENCH PHILOSOPHER

Chapter 1

$\mathcal{T}$he back of my neck tingled with the sense of someone looking at me. Mike.

I was starting to turn around when Jessie Tate interrupted me.

"Will you check my problems, Anna?" she asked, clutching a notebook, catching herself as the bus rocked through a mud hole.

I patted the seat beside me where somebody had inked *Maverick* into the brown leather.

"Preacher says it's wicked to stay home and watch *Maverick* on Sunday night," Jessie announced, thrusting her notebook into my lap.

Well, we didn't have a television so I didn't have to worry about that particular sin.

I glanced at Jessie's homework. "Look," I said, pointing to a couple of problems. "You have to do the math inside the parentheses first. Remember? Always start on the inside and work your way out."

"Oh yeah." She took the notebook back and attacked her work, erased, blew and brushed the rubbings onto my skirt.

As Jessie worked, I took out the new glasses that I still forgot about sometimes. Carolyn said glasses were boy bait—that boys fantasized about taking off girls' glasses—which made no sense to me at all.

The rims were black, with three little rhinestones in each corner, almost identical to the kind Meema had worn.

"Now look," Jessie said, tilting her notebook so I could see the reworked answers.

I scanned them. "They're fine, Jessie."

"Thanks!" She slapped the notebook shut and bounded forward to her seat.

I opened my trig book to read the problem I had to explain in class that morning. But before I could begin, Mike moved up to my seat.

"Hi," he said. "Mind if I sit with you?"

Mind?

I smiled at him and he settled in beside me. He wore a pair of black wash pants and a plaid shirt, and I could smell the Niagara starch as if the shirt were still warm from the ironing board.

"What are you working on?" he asked.

Before I could stop myself, I spread my fingers over the open pages.

He leaned over to read the page anyway. "Trigonometry?" he asked, brushing my fingers aside. I could see little comb tracks in the hair behind his ear.

"No. I mean *yes*. It's a math review problem I have to present in trig class."

"You have to show the class how to solve it?"

I nodded.

"Show me."

"Now?"

"Yeah," he said.

I read the problem in a low voice, my face burning. Mr. Walters had the bus heater up way too high. If Carolyn heard about me reading math to a boy, she'd never let me forget it. The first rule of boy-girl etiquette: Never make a boy feel you're smarter than he is.

But while I sketched the diagram, Mike leaned close,

watching, his arm touching mine. "So a railroad track goes around a curve and you have to find out how much longer the outside rail is than the inside one," he remarked when I held the drawing up.

I nodded.

"Will you go to Homecoming with me?" he asked.

My pencil started shaking so I slid it into the spiral of my notebook, closed everything up, and stacked the books neatly on my lap. Then I turned my face ninety degrees and looked into Mike's eyes. They were brown and widely spaced—the calmest eyes I'd ever seen.

"Just you?" I asked.

"Well, yeah." Mike laughed.

I had said something incredibly stupid. "I don't think so."

He frowned.

"It's just that I can't go in a car alone with a boy until I'm sixteen."

"Why not?"

"It's a rule. My daddy says I have to wait until then."

"Well, is that a long way off? Being sixteen?" Hope rose in Mike's eyes.

"Next April."

"Oh."

I looked away, turning my pencil inside the spiral.

But he rallied. "Your daddy will need to bend the rules this once because Homecoming will be all over by next April."

I laughed at his twist of logic. He didn't understand that Daddy's rules were like mathematics axioms. Bend an axiom and the whole universe collapsed.

As we rode along on the bus, Mike didn't say anything for a while. He had opened a notebook with unlined sheets of paper and he sketched things we saw out the bus windows. Rolling fields, nearly bare trees, the great wooden skeleton of the railroad overpass across Skillet Fork.

"Meema was an artist," I said.

"Who's Meema?"

"My grandmother. She was killed in an accident last Fourth of July." Mike might have heard about it, even though it had happened before his family moved here.

He looked up from his work. "I'm sorry," he said, and I saw in his eyes that he was.

Meema's death had slammed shut a part of the past that was precious to me. For a few years during World

War II, I had lived with Meema and Granddad. Then, after the war, when Daddy came back and we set up our own home, I continued to stay at Meema's a lot of the time. I still had my own bedroom there.

In Mike's drawing, the very school bus in which we rode emerged on the far side of Skillet Fork. Then he ripped the sheet out of his notebook. "Would you like to have this? In exchange for the trig problem?"

"Thanks."

And now it was my turn again. I took his pencil and wrote the number 220 neatly in the corner of a page of his sketch pad. Then I penciled 284 in very small letters in the lower right-hand corner of the drawing he'd given me.

"They're friendly numbers that have a mystical relationship with each other," I heard myself saying.

Our eyes met, and Mike smiled.

Mrs. Ballard had told us about Pythagoras's friendly numbers. They were equal to the sum of the other's proper divisors. The proper divisors of 220 were 1, 2, 4, 5, 10, 11, 20, 22, 44, 55, and 110. And those numbers summed to 284. And 284's proper divisors summed to 220.

We were at school then and I saw Carolyn out front in the cold, hugging her books and stamping her feet, waiting for me.

"Just ask your daddy," Mike said as he followed me down the bus steps.

Chapter 2

"Perfect, Anna," Mr. Carson declared, as I finished presenting the problem of the railroad tracks.

Nate rolled his eyes at me, communicating what all the boys in trig class thought. A girl with some mathematical ability was like a poodle that could do cute tricks: charming, but of no real value in their world.

All except for Bud Keegan.

The Keegans lived up the road north of us in nothing more than a dugout. Five kids and no mother. And Bud did his homework in tiny print on both sides of the paper clear out to the margins—paper so worn that I hated touching it when we checked each other's work. But Bud's math grades were almost as good as mine and he treated me like a friend instead of a novelty item.

"Anna has taken us almost halfway to the solution of today's real problem—which is, how much track could we save if we laid it in a straight line from one end of the curve to the other?" He turned the chalk sideways and drew a thick line straight between the endpoints of the curve.

We would have to find the length of that line and compare it with the length of the curve. I looked at the board and tried to picture what to do before Mr. Carson mapped it all out. We would have to come up with two right angles and use the sine function.

But the catch turned out to be that we had to find the sine of half a twenty-five-degree angle, which—of course—wasn't in the tables in the back of the book. I averaged the values of twelve and thirteen degrees and came up with an answer which, in this case, turned out to be right.

However, averaging wouldn't always work, as Mr. Carson explained, because sometimes the angle you were looking for wasn't exactly halfway between the two listed in the table. *And* you had to consider whether the sine was rising or falling.

So, he had introduced us to interpolation—which seemed simple enough—even if it did mean grinding out a lot of numbers with our pencils.

During the whole class, Mr. Carson's slide rule lay on his desk. I would have given anything for a slide rule. Maybe if Daddy hadn't had to buy my glasses I could have talked him into one for Christmas. A slide rule would be much faster and easier than using tables in a book.

When class was dismissed for lunch I stayed at my desk, waiting for Carolyn, who was in a room down the hall taking a timed typing test. Carolyn had aspirations to be the fastest typist, the best dictation taker, and the most fashionable secretary in North America. She would eventually marry the boss—who looked a lot like Rock Hudson—and he would keep her well with a house in Connecticut, a station wagon, a houseful of children, and a beagle.

Carolyn could style her thick strawberry blond hair three different ways in ten minutes. And I loved her because she looked right through my oddness without even seeing it.

Chapter 3

"Where's Daddy?" I asked, dropping my books on the kitchen counter.

"I expect he's working late," Mama replied. "Why?"

She was ironing in the kitchen, a basket of sprinkled and rolled laundry beside her. The twins' tiny starched dresses hung from the cupboard knobs. Mama was listening to Bobby Darin singing "Mack the Knife" on KXOK.

"I need to ask him something," I said.

I poured a glass of milk and took a handful of Saltines into the dining room. The east window was open. The twins played at the edge of the yard, digging in a pile of dirt left over from plowing. The bottoms of their red dresses ruffled out like poppies beneath their long sweaters.

Over by the barn, a cow bawled for her calf.

The twins looked up, saw me, and flew to the window.

"We're digging a cave, Anna!" Melanie announced in her croaky bullfrog voice.

"And we'll live in it when it's done!" Cassie chimed in, brandishing a sandbox shovel.

The girls giggled and ran back to their excavation site.

"What did you want to ask Daddy?" Mama said as I returned to the kitchen to rinse my glass.

I didn't want to talk about it twice. Asking Daddy would be hard enough, especially when I knew he was going to say no.

"Anna?" Mama pressed.

I sighed. "Mike Dillon asked me to the Homecoming game."

"Just the two of you?"

"Yes." I felt my face turning hot.

"Well, I think that would be real nice," Mama said. "But—"

"You've been so blue since—" She broke off to shake out my plaid skirt before she spread it over the ironing board, and she didn't finish the sentence. It would have ended *since Meema died.* "It'll do you good to get out. Besides, Mike's just a neighbor."

But being turned loose to go out alone with a boy wasn't supposed to happen yet. Sixteen was a *number.* An integer. And I wouldn't be that number for more than five months. Mama, of all people, should know that.

"Isn't the Homecoming game a week from Friday?" she asked.

I nodded.

"Then this Saturday we could go into town and shop for something pretty for you to wear. We could take Carolyn and make a day of it. Wouldn't that be fun? We could leave the twins at home with Daddy."

Mama took the twins everywhere. They were her life. When I was little, she'd been away, living and working where Daddy was stationed during the war, and I'd grown up as Meema's girl. I knew it wasn't Mama's fault Meema had died, but I wished she wouldn't try to horn in now.

I could hear the strain in her voice, as I'm sure she could hear it in mine when I said, "I guess I could mention it to Carolyn."

Mama had no more than started passing the pot

roast around that evening when Daddy said to me, "So you want to go out with Mike Dillon just this one time?"

His eyebrows stayed up as he waited for my answer.

Yes would sound like I wanted to go one time. *No* would sound like I didn't want to go at all.

Boolean algebra, where every answer was yes or no, one or zero, on or off, wasn't working.

And while I struggled, Daddy made up his mind. "I guess it would be okay this once."

Chapter 4

When we were carving pumpkins on the front porch the next evening, I hugged my knees under my skirt, trying to keep warm.

The paper Mr. Carson had given us rustled in my skirt pocket. I took it out.

"What's that?" Daddy asked.

"An invitation," I said, not knowing where to begin.

"An invitation?"

"To a math contest at the university. In the spring."

Daddy's eyes showed puzzlement.

"I'd like to go."

Daddy frowned as he went back to working on Cassie's pumpkin. "Why?" he asked.

"Well, I'll be out of high school in one year," I said. *Some* people went to college, though nobody in our family had yet.

"What do you think I'll be when I grow up?" I asked.

Daddy stopped carving the snaggletooth grin on Cassie's pumpkin and looked at me as if I'd asked from which direction the sun would rise tomorrow. "Well, I expect you'll be a fine wife and mother."

I sighed.

"If you can find a good man to take care of you, you don't need to *be* anything."

I buried my face in the crook of my arm so Daddy wouldn't see my expression.

"Sometimes things can go wrong with a plan like that," he conceded. "There's Mrs. Ballard, for instance."

His mouth curved down as if he'd said *There's leprosy, for instance.*

Did he know what he was saying? Mrs. Ballard had two degrees in math. She made it come alive—to seem like something more important than just finding solutions to textbook problems.

Mrs. Ballard was divorced. That's what Daddy meant. She wasn't respectable. A math and science teacher, of all things! And real lucky to have a job, as he was very fond of pointing out, since she was a divorced woman.

"It wouldn't hurt to have a backup plan," Daddy admitted. "Secretarial courses would be good."

Sometimes Daddy sounded just like Carolyn. Learn to type and marry the boss.

"But you find a good man, Anna, and the future will take care of itself." He fitted the top on Cassie's pumpkin.

I missed Meema so much. She would have looked Daddy in the eye and said, "Let Anna try out her dreams. She's different."

I snatched up my knife and went to work on my pumpkin.

"Yours looks really mad, Anna," Melanie said after we had lined the jack-o'-lanterns up on the porch railing.

And although it was a school night, and Daddy surely knew I had homework, he asked me to ride up to Granddad's with him as soon as supper was over. "I need to take back the come-along," he explained. "Dad's still got a few cows that haven't calved yet."

"Go on, Anna," Mama encouraged me. "The twins and I can do the dishes."

I didn't want to go to Granddad's house. It was too painful.

"Dad's not seen you for a long time," Daddy said, playing on my guilt.

When Meema died, Granddad had lost me as well. I'd always spent a lot of time up there, staying in my old room upstairs next to Meema's workroom. The bus driver was used to me flagging him down in front of their house.

"Tell Granddad I'll see him at church on Sunday," I said. I'd been using headaches, cramps, head colds, and anything I could think of to get out of going to church. But maybe Daddy would take the hook: I'd go to church Sunday if he wouldn't make me go to Granddad's tonight.

"You come on," Daddy insisted. "I need some company."

I got my jacket and followed him, but I banged the truck door so hard that the puff of dust made me cough. The come-along rattled in the back as we jolted over the rough road. If I had to go to Meema and Granddad's house, then Daddy had to listen to me about going to visit the university.

That was my real motive for competing in the

math contest. Who cared about another test? My whole experience of college campuses came from a movie I'd gone to with Meema and Granddad.

College would be easier to talk Daddy into if I'd touched and smelled it first.

"So can I go?" I asked.

Daddy knew what I meant—what I'd been sitting there thinking about.

"Don't you reckon you need to rest that mind of yours now and then? Give it some time off from all that schoolwork?"

"My mind isn't tired."

Daddy didn't say any more.

When we got to Granddad's, there was a light on in the kitchen, and the rest of the place was dark.

I went in while Daddy took the come-along to the machine shed. My stomach hurt.

"Anna!" Granddad said, looking up.

His pale, bald forehead gleamed in the overhead light. Fried potatoes and meat were half eaten on a plate, and the house smelled of old grease. Dishes, dirty and clean, littered the counters.

"Where have you been?" he tried to tease. "I thought maybe you'd moved away."

I gave him a hug and stretched out my hand to the rambling bittersweet painted on the cupboards.

"Meema did that," he said, as if I might have forgotten in four months the very essence of her and all the beauty she brought to our world.

The harsh overhead light that Granddad had on was unkind to all that beauty. When Meema was alive, she used soft lamplight even in the kitchen.

What emptiness lay beyond the glare of the kitchen, I couldn't bear to think about. My old room upstairs.

We didn't stay long. Granddad offered to fry us some tenderloin, but Daddy told him we'd had supper.

"You should eat with us, Dad," Daddy said as we were leaving. "Jo has said a hundred times she'd be glad to have you."

Granddad murmured something, but he shook his head no.

On the way back home, I stared into the blackness, knowing exactly what was out there. Corn stubble, timber, rusted and abandoned oil pumps.

Daddy tapped his hand on the steering wheel. "Anna, I'm letting you go out with a boy, even though you're not sixteen yet. I can understand a girl wanting to do that."

Why was Daddy talking about my date with Mike?

"And now you're asking me to let you make a trip to the university. *That* I don't understand."

At least Daddy was still thinking about it.

But my hopefulness didn't last long, because he said, "A trip to visit the university just seems like a waste of time to me."

I left it there. At least he hadn't said definitely no.

Chapter 5

Friday, after school, I dropped my books on the desk in the living room.

"Are you home, Anna?" Mama called.

"Yes."

"Would you like a roast beef sandwich?"

I could no more eat than I could swallow that Russian Sputnik everybody was so worried about. My stomach made a gurgling sound.

"I'm not hungry," I said.

Mama stood in the kitchen doorway, drying her hands. "Are you excited? About your first real date?"

I nodded, glancing away, not wanting her to see just how excited.

I'd gone with Carolyn and two boys and a parent chaperone to play miniature golf last spring. I'd gone with Marvin Richardson, a short kid who played drums in the band, and his parents to a movie a couple of times. But going to the game with Mike was really a date.

As I ran water in the tub, I stripped off my school clothes and slipped into a housecoat.

After my bath, I got out the makeup kit that Aunt Susie had sent me from California last Christmas. I stared at the untouched disk of powder; at the promising precision of the eyebrow pencil; at the smoothness of the lipstick.

I fumbled with the strange tools for making myself beautiful.

A few minutes later, Melanie and Cassie drifted into the bathroom. "What'cha doing?" one asked.

"Making an eyebrow." My face had a lopsided aspect because my other eyebrow was still sun-bleached and pale. And my nose looked dark from the powder.

The twins scrambled up on the clothes hamper for a better view. I drew a second eyebrow.

"You look like a bunny," Cassie whispered.

I sketched in whiskers on my upper lip and turned

to the twins, wiggling my nose. Cassie shrieked and jumped off the hamper.

"Do me." Melanie turned up her face.

By the time the headlights of Mike's car reflected off my bedroom wall, I'd given up on the makeup and just scrubbed my face, brushed my hair, and dressed. I rubbed a last bit of Pacquin's lotion into my hands. In the living room, the twins, both painted like rabbits, sat side by side on the couch in their pink pajamas.

Holding my jacket, I waited. What was taking Mike so long? Then I heard his footsteps on the porch. I jumped when he knocked.

Mike's eyes shone. His dark hair looked freshly cut. As he stepped in, he carried a fan of damp leaves on his shoe, which I tried not to look at.

"Hello, Mike," Mama called from the kitchen doorway. "Did your mother get her dahlias dug up?"

Mike nodded. "Yes, ma'am, I guess so." Mike glanced at Daddy, who was sitting on the couch beside the twins. Daddy peered at Mike over the top of the newspaper for a moment, then stood up. As Mike stepped toward Daddy, he felt the leaves under his foot and looked down. "Sorry," he murmured.

"I'll get the—" We bent down at the same time,

bumping into each other. "Let me get them," I said, picking them up.

Mike was blushing when he shook hands with Daddy.

"Have Anna home by ten-thirty."

"Yes, sir."

I felt my face burning too.

Mike looked so different than he did on the bus. So tall. His sweater was an olive drab that made his dark hair and eyes stand out.

"Bye," I said, waving at the twins, who stared word-lessly.

"Good night," Mike called, helping me on with my coat and blessedly closing the door behind us.

Chapter 6

The cool darkness was such a relief that I laughed. I let loose of the handful of wet leaves from Mike's shoe, then slid my hand in my pocket to wipe off my fingers.

"There's Orion's belt." His voice sounded different. It had a timbre that made him seem more familiar. Intimate. Like a friend. Like Carolyn's voice when we slept at each other's houses.

"I see it," I said.

Mike helped me into the car. As he walked around to his side I adjusted my clothing, stirring up the smell of Mama's Fabergé cologne that I had dabbed in the crooks of my arms.

I fingered the small piece of paper in my pocket. I'd written a list of things to talk about. *Sports, Mike's old school, his family, the best kind of cookies, the weather, the Thanksgiving holiday, pets.* I had the list memorized.

"Do you suppose we'll win the game tonight?" Mike asked as we turned out of the driveway.

A sports question. The same as the first item on my list.

I told him I didn't know. Honestly, I didn't even know who our team was playing.

"Why didn't you go out for basketball?" I asked.

Mike was tall, with square shoulders and long legs. In our tiny school, every able-bodied boy put on the blue and gold.

"My old school had a lot of guys who were good. So I didn't even think about it."

"How many kids went to your old school?"

"About five hundred."

Our school had only about eighty students. Bud, Nate, and I were the only ones in Mrs. Ballard's geometry class.

"I'll bet you even had a football team," I marveled. "And a marching band."

"Yeah," Mike said.

"Do you miss it?"

"Not a whole lot. I like living in the country. But where we used to live, I could walk to the movies. I went every week if I could come up with the money. I guess that's something I miss."

"Why did you all move here anyway?" I asked.

"The stove factory where Dad worked closed. His cousin from Mills City said he'd heard a house out in the country was for rent pretty cheap. And he thought he could get Dad on at the shoe factory in Baxter."

"Is your daddy going to farm in the spring?"

"He doesn't know how to farm," Mike said. "He's from Chicago. But Mom says we're going to put in a garden. She's not from Chicago. She's from Kentucky."

I'd met Mike's mother back in September when Mama invited her to the Ladies Aid meeting at our house. Mrs. Dillon was tall and thin with pale red hair—very pretty—but when she smiled, decayed teeth marred her beauty. She talked in a softer way than we did around here.

"I remember the first time I saw you," I told Mike. "I was driving the hay wagon by your place in August when you were mowing."

"I'd seen you before that," he said. "We came to look at the Lowry place back in June. When we drove by your house, you were out in the yard swinging."

I wished Mike's first impression hadn't been of me doing something childish.

"You jumped out of the swing," he went on. "And you went flying through the air. You looked so happy—like you might just bounce right up into the sky."

That would have been before Meema's accident. Sometimes I couldn't even remember having once been so happy.

I could see Mike's hand on the wheel, his long fingers, and the glint of an ID bracelet at the edge of his sweater sleeve.

The first three things on my list—sports, Mike's old school, and his family—were used up and we weren't even to the highway yet.

"That's a pretty sweater you're wearing."

"Thank you." It was a pink lamb's wool that Mama had bought me the Saturday she and Carolyn and I had gone shopping for this very occasion.

Mike's hand left the wheel and he leaned forward, reaching for something on the floor. He held out a cube-shaped box to me, its whiteness glowing in the dashboard lights.

The box weighed practically nothing, but something shifted inside. "What is it?" I asked.

"Something to put on your sweater," he said.

Mike had gotten me a corsage. It was too dark in the car to see, so I held the box to my nose, sniffing. The cool fragrance of roses.

"Thank you."

"You're welcome." After a pause, Mike asked, "Who painted the pictures in your living room?"

I'd seen him looking, as everybody did who came to our house for the first time.

"My grandmother that I told you about. Meema."

"Wow! They're good." Then he added, "They're more than good. They make you feel like you're seeing the world differently. I wish I could do that."

Sometimes when I really looked at Meema's paintings—looked at them freshly and deeply—they almost brought her back.

"Where did you learn to draw?" I asked Mike.

"No place. I just know how, like my mom. Her mom, Gran Day in Kentucky, carves dolls that look as real as living babies. We have a whole shelf of them. My mom sewed their clothes. Maybe I can show you sometime. Maybe your little sisters would get a kick out of seeing the dolls."

"I'll bet they would," I said, smiling. I'd never have thought of putting dolls on my list of things to talk to Mike about. I guess Mama and Carolyn were right. There were a million things, after all.

Chapter 7

At school, the lights blazed. People who'd graduated a few years earlier drifted through the halls—some of the women wearing short, stylish mouton jackets that made them look like movie stars.

Mike and I followed the crowd through the central corridor. From the gym, the buzzer sounded, followed by the pounding of feet down the floor. The B-team cheerleaders began a chant and then the long end-of-game buzzer blared from the gym.

"I guess the JV game is over," Mike said.

"I'll go put on my corsage," I told him.

In the girls' bathroom, Becky Harris, one of the A-team cheerleaders, was changing into her uniform.

When I lifted the lid of the corsage box, I saw a cluster of white rosebuds with a twist of bittersweet caught in the ribbon. Bittersweet.

"You must really like it," Becky said, sounding amused as she adjusted her sweater. "I heard Mike Dillon asked you out."

I nodded, touching the bittersweet.

"I know some cheerleaders who'd like to date him," Becky said. "Do you need help with that?" She pointed to the corsage.

"Probably," I admitted as a group of freshmen came through the door.

Becky lifted the flowers out of the box and turned me to face the full-length mirror.

"Pret-ty," one of the girls cooed, looking at the corsage in the mirror.

"Thanks," I said.

Becky removed a long, pearl-tipped pin from the back of the corsage and fastened the flowers to my sweater.

"Who gave you that?" one of the girls asked.

"Mike Dillon."

I saw the glance the girls exchanged as I walked out the door.

"Have fun," Becky said, brushing past me, her skirt swaying over her bare legs.

Mike leaned against the locker, his back to me.

The hallway, so familiar in the daytime, seemed foreign at night. The school band played from the gym and the smell of popcorn curled through the crowd.

"Do you want anything?" Mike asked, as we passed the concession stand.

Mrs. Ballard, my geometry teacher, caught my eye and smiled as she filled a popcorn box. The Future Homemakers of America girls were selling home-made fudge.

"Hey, Mike," Carolyn called from the concession stand. "Anna's supposed to be helping us. Did you know that?"

The girls in the FHA booth looked at us, watching to see what Mike might say.

"No, ma'am," Mike called to Carolyn. "I didn't know that."

"But she had a *daaate*," Carolyn said, drawing out the word. "So she was excused."

As the girls giggled, I decided I would never speak to Carolyn Jackson again.

"How can I make it up to you?" Mike asked Carolyn.

She blinked. "What?"

"How can I make it up to you—depriving you of Anna and all?"

One of the girls whispered something in Carolyn's ear. "Buy a whole pan of fudge," Carolyn declared, triumph on her face.

I saw an expression flicker in Mike's eyes. "How much does that cost?"

The girls conferred for a second. "A dollar," Carolyn announced.

"Okay," Mike said, getting out his billfold.

The girl cutting the fudge held up her spatula. "What can we put it in?"

I was so relieved Mike didn't mind donating a dollar to the FHA that I babbled, "I'll get my corsage box. We can use that."

We then went into the gym, finding seats at the far end, near the cheerleaders. Becky wiggled her fingers at me.

I didn't know or care a thing about basketball, but following the cheerleaders' chants was fun. I clapped until my hands smarted.

By the end of the first quarter, my lips were dry. I wished I hadn't left my Tangee in my jacket pocket.

When the halftime buzzer sounded, Mike went to get us Cokes. I saved his seat, watching the cheerleaders make their pyramids in the middle of the gym floor.

Halftime was nearly over when Mike finally came through the crowd. He held a Coke bottle in each hand. "Lines," he said.

The coldness of the ridged Coke bottle was painful on my pink, swollen palms.

"No straws," Mike said. "They're all gone."

I shut my eyes and tilted my head back. "Thank you," I breathed after a few gulps.

Mike laughed. "Good, huh?"

The game went on, the buzzer now and then letting a blast rip into the commotion. Mike's arms and mine bumped sometimes when we clapped, jumped up to cheer, and sat back down. After the third quarter, four of the varsity cheerleaders slipped out. They were going to the Home Ec room to put on their formals.

Finally, with only a few seconds left, the crowd stood silent, watching one of our team at the free-throw line. The ball arced into the basket. The crowd cheered and the final buzzer sounded.

"Don't go away!" the principal commanded over the public address system. "Give the band a minute to set up. Then we'll have the crowning of the Luster Community Consolidated High School Homecoming Queen, nineteen fifty-nine, Miss Mary Middleton!"

Chapter 8

"If we leave by ten, we'll be okay," Mike said, looking at the clock.

We had nineteen minutes. I willed the visiting fans who were emptying the bleachers to *hurry*.

The band, five guys in sport jackets, set up their equipment at the foot of the stage. The drummer made an adjustment on the snare and tapped a few measures.

Seventeen minutes. Mike kept glancing at the clock too.

Just then, the curtains on the stage opened, the lights dimmed, and the band began to play. A spotlight flitted around the gym.

When we were quiet, the principal announced, "Ladies and gentlemen, the queen's court!"

We clapped as a little girl in a formal, wearing a tiny tiara, dragged a small crew-cut boy in a suit into the spotlight. With the other hand she flung rose petals into the air.

The queen's court floated down the purple runner that ran the length of the gym. Some of the girls had dusted their hair with glitter, and it caught the spotlight.

"Look!" I touched Mike's leg, forgetting for a second that he wasn't Carolyn. "There's Becky! She helped with my corsage."

Finally, the band surged into "So Rare" as we all rose to our feet, applauding, over the principal intoning, "The nineteen fifty-nine Homecoming Queen!"

Mary Middleton strolled the length of the gym on the arm of the captain of the basketball team as people flung carnations and confetti onto the floor.

"Isn't she pretty? Don't you love her formal?" I blurted out.

I pounded my hands together.

Mary climbed the steps and turned, sending the skirt of her formal out in a lavender billow. She took her place on the velvet-draped throne, then held her arms out for the long-stemmed red roses. Behind her, a backdrop of silver stars sparkled against a midnight-purple sky.

Cameras fired little bursts of blue light at people on the stage. Mike tugged my arm, leading me through the crowd. The burned-plastic smell of spent flash-bulbs floated around us.

I glanced at the clock on the gym wall. Nine fifty-nine.

We grabbed our jackets and cut out the east door, which was less crowded. The October cold made me suck in my breath. Mike took a shortcut across the grass in the dark, coming out on the grade-school playground. Flagpole chains chimed in the breeze.

The corsage made a lump under my jacket as we ran into the wind.

When we got to the car, Mike opened the door for me.

Before I got in, I turned to Mike. "Why is there bittersweet in my corsage? The other girls had baby's breath."

"It grows up the side of our garage, so I asked my mom to take out that white stuff and put in the bittersweet. Everybody wants the white stuff. I think you're different."

And Mike kissed me right there when I wasn't expecting it.

I shut my eyes and felt his breath on my face. Finding his hand, I twined my fingers through his.

On the way home, I suggested the fudge, my voice not quite steady.

"Yeah," he said. "I'm starved."

After he'd taken a piece, I bit into one, letting the sugar dissolve on my tongue.

We were in our own world. Our own private space. Mike had the heater on and it stirred the smell of chocolate and our wool clothing.

"Do you think your daddy might let you go to a movie with me? There's a good one coming to the Stadium next weekend."

"I'll ask him."

When we pulled into our drive, the lamp in the picture window glowed through the white draperies.

Mike turned on the overhead light and neatened what was left of the fudge in the corsage box and put the lid on. Then he flipped off the light.

"Give this to your mom," he said, pressing the box

into my hands, shaping my fingers around it, and holding them there for a few seconds.

I waited for him to come around and help me out.

"Good night," he said on the porch. His hands clasped my arms, and this time I was ready for the kiss.

But Mama opened the door. "Goodness!" she exclaimed. "It's gotten colder."

"Good night," Mike said again, speaking to Mama, dropping his hands to his sides.

"Thanks," I called to his back as he headed for the car.

Inside, I handed Mama the white box. "Mike gave me this for you."

Her face showed her confusion as she felt the weight of the box.

"Open it."

"Fudge! Nobody has ever given me a box of fudge."

"And look at the corsage," I said, brushing the rosebuds with my fingers.

"Oh, Anna, how pretty! You can put it in your keepsake box."

In my room, I arranged the corsage on the table beside my bed.

When I finally turned off the light and stretched out in the darkness, I still heard the crowd cheering, and my fingers twitched a little as they lay folded across my stomach.

I turned on my side and touched the roses. My parents murmured a few words across the hall and then fell silent.

Eventually, too jangled to sleep, I got up and put on Meema's gold charm bracelet. Granddad had brought it down to me a few weeks after she died. I had never actually worn it before, so my wrist felt strange wrapped in the gold links.

Chapter 9

$\mathcal{S}$unday morning Daddy said *No excuses*. So I went to church.

Instead of following my family to the front as usual, I slid into one of the pews just inside the sanctuary door where the young people sat.

Mary Anderson moved over to make a place for me.

Daddy finally figured out I was missing and turned around. When his eyes found me in the young people's section, he smiled.

Things looked so different from here. I couldn't see the altar table. The painting of Jesus in the Garden of Gethsemane had a glare on it.

Mary's older sister, Christine, made her way down the aisle to where the young marrieds sat. Christine shifted her baby in her arms and turned to say something to her husband. Ralph took the baby briefly while Christine shrugged out of her jacket.

She'd had to get married two summers ago before her senior year of high school.

"Ralph has a job at Kroger's now," Mary said. "In the produce department. They're real happy." She wiggled her fingers at the rosy-faced boy who smiled over his mama's shoulder. Then she leaned toward me. "Christine is expecting again."

"That's nice," I said.

The little boy played peekaboo with us over his mama's shoulder.

Christine and Ralph had nothing to be ashamed of this time. But two summers ago, when the rumors started, Mary had looked pale and sad and thin, with circles beneath her downcast eyes. And I'd felt sorry for their whole family. I couldn't imagine being in Christine's shoes.

One Sunday, the preacher had announced that Christine and Ralph were married. *At least he married her* is what people said then. But that didn't remove the shame. Forever and ever, people might love Christine and her first little boy, but they'd remember that she'd gotten pregnant before she was married. And that disgrace smeared Christine's whole family. It made people wonder what was wrong with her parents that their daughter did such a thing. It made people wonder if Mary would be just like her.

The piano player began "What a Friend We Have in Jesus." I hadn't noticed Granddad come in, but there he was beside Daddy. Now both Meema and I were missing from our pew.

As we stood to sing, I felt penned in, staring at the backs of the young marrieds. So I was glad to escape downstairs for Sunday school.

I tried to be attentive in class, but the metal folding chair seemed hard and cold, and I shifted, crossing one leg and then the other.

On my turn to read a Bible verse, Mary had to nudge me, and I mechanically produced the words.

"And what does that mean?" our teacher asked.

I looked at the verse again. The best I could offer was something safe that fit every verse in the New Testament. "That we need God's love."

And nobody must know that I didn't have it, or at

least couldn't feel it. Unquestioning faith was like virginity. If I got caught without it, I would shame Meema, Granddad, my parents, the twins, and all the cows on our farm.

After class, on the way back to the sanctuary, Mary elbowed me. "I hear you went to a basketball game with a boy."

How did Mary know that? We didn't go to the same high school. Mary lived in the next township north.

"You should invite him to church," she said.

If I invited Mike to church, maybe it would take my mind off everything that was missing.

Part 2: Winter

Sophie Germain, born in France in 1776, taught herself calculus and number theory from the books in her father's library. This unfeminine behavior worried her parents and they fiercely discouraged her interest. Sophie gained access to university mathematics by adopting the persona of a man. When her reputation in the mathematical community was established, she revealed herself as a woman and went on to make an important breakthrough in the proving of Fermat's Last Theorem.

Chapter 10

The schedule Mrs. Myers had taped to the wall said everybody should have finished cutting out their garments by today, December 16. How long had I been separating the individual pattern pieces from the big, unwieldy sheets of tissue paper? How long had I been folding, laying out, and pinning?

And even now it didn't look quite right.

Nobody asked Carolyn to prove the Pythagorean Theorem or Bud to type eighty words a minute or Mike to sing *Aida*. So why did I have to make a garment in Home Ec?

I had a feeling like in those terrible dreams where, no matter what you do, you can't find the right doorway to the bathroom or get the burning cake out of the oven.

Sunshine washed over the table in the Home Ec room where Carolyn and I had our patterns laid out. I was the only one who hadn't finished cutting except for her, and she dawdled out of loyalty. Before Mike, Carolyn might have abandoned me to go off and make her neat, straight seams. But now she paid a sort of funny homage to my new status as Mike Dillon's girlfriend.

I stared at the pattern pieces for my simple blouse. Girls were supposed to know how to do such things.

The snow light filled the room with a harsh glare, giving me a headache.

Carolyn cut slowly. But she was down to her last piece of rust-colored paisley print, which she was making into an entire shirtwaist dress with set-in sleeves, a lapel collar, a front placket, a zipper, side pockets, a pleated skirt, and a fabric belt.

I had picked up the scissors and begun to hack around one of the pattern pieces when Mrs. Myers came over to our table. "About done?" she asked us.

"I guess," Carolyn admitted, brushing the last of her scraps into the wastebasket. And she went off to the sewing machines, leaving me to face Mrs. Myers alone.

I pushed up my sweater sleeves and stared at the pink cotton.

Mrs. Myers slipped a pair of shears out of her smock pocket. "Let's work together," she offered.

Her shears made patient, rhythmic slicing sounds and a neat edge of tissue paper fell away to the right.

Working from the other side of the table, I tried to imitate her, struggling to follow the solid lines on the pattern. The broken line inside the solid line was the place where I was expected to *stitch*. My temples throbbed at the prospect.

In the corner, sewing machines whirred, their pitch rising and falling with their speed.

"Pink is a nice color," Mrs. Myers remarked. "And you'll be able to wear a simple blouse like this lots of places."

It wouldn't be fit to wear to a dog fight, as Daddy would say. I planned to cram it in the back of a drawer and throw it away as soon as Mama forgot about the almost three dollars she had invested in fabric, pattern, and thread.

As I snipped around the curve of the front armhole

facing, Mrs. Myers said, "I'll be starting my home visits soon. Right after Christmas vacation. I'm looking forward to visiting with your mother."

On the tight curve of the Peter Pan collar, the tissue paper kept creeping across the fabric despite all my pins.

Just as I finished the piece, thank God the timer buzzed on one of the ovens that Mrs. Myers set to ring five minutes in advance of the bell.

"Cleanup time," she called.

Out of the graciousness of her heart, she finished cutting the bodice back. "There," she said, sliding the pieces across the table to me. "You're on schedule again."

After school, on the bus, I sat by Mike. My feet were icy from the wet slush I'd waded through. I hugged my armful of books to stop the shivers, wishing Mr. Walters could turn up the heater. I wanted to snuggle up to Mike, but settled for a long, warming look into his eyes.

Carolyn said Mike and I probably didn't kiss, that we just gazed at each other. She was fishing for information, and even though she was my best friend, I wasn't about to tell her how close Mike and I had become.

Mike ripped out a drawing and handed it to me. I tucked it inside my notebook.

"What do you do with them all?" he asked.

"Honestly?" I felt my face turning pink. "I keep them folded inside the sweater I wore on our first date."

"Yeah?"

He looked so ridiculously pleased that I had to laugh.

When he got off the bus, he said, "Two twenty," as always.

"Two eighty-four," I answered.

That day back in October when I'd told Mike about the friendly numbers seemed like such a long time ago.

Chapter 11

That night, I borrowed Mama's flared coat with the black velvet collar and large velvet buttons down the front.

The minute the door closed behind us we linked fingers, and when we were halfway down the sidewalk, Mike stopped and pulled me to him. My arms slid inside his open coat. He was so warm. We kissed until I finally stepped away.

"Daddy may be listening for the car to start," I whispered.

I sensed Mike's smile in the darkness.

For the last two months, Daddy had let me go out with Mike whenever I asked, apparently reasoning that a boy was less danger to me than too much math.

In Baxter, when we turned north at the four-way stop, a line wound from the movie theater, up the block, and past the funeral home.

Mike found a parking place in front of the old Hamilton Hotel. "Look at all those people," he said. "I hope we can get in."

We attached ourselves to the end of the long line.

The wind on my neck made me shiver. When I clutched my coat collar under my chin, I smelled Mama's powder and hair spray. She'd left a handkerchief in her pocket, and I explored its starched and ironed folds with my fingers.

Mike pounded his gloved hands together and blew out an explosion of frosty breath. We inched along in the line, our arms bumping. I loved the rolling white lights around the edge of the Stadium marquee. *Anatomy of a Murder* must be a wonderful movie to draw such a crowd.

My feet and legs were aching with cold as Mike finally paid the $1.40 and we got our tickets and stepped into the warm lobby.

A cream Thunderbird convertible with a glowing red interior gleamed in the spotlight as it rotated on a turntable.

"Buy the pretty little lady a raffle ticket?" a man in a houndstooth sport jacket asked.

We just hurried past him into the darkness of the theater. The short subject had already started.

"There's not much left," an usher whispered, his red jacket catching the light of the flickering movie screen. "You got the first row or the top of the balcony."

"Balcony," Mike said.

The usher flicked his flashlight over the steps, leading us upward. Then he spotlighted the two empty seats for us.

"Excuse me," I murmured, stepping in front of people.

Mike settled in beside me.

The cartoon was a Woody Woodpecker, Granddad's favorite. I'd often gone to movies with Meema and Granddad on Saturday nights when they went to town to buy groceries. What was Granddad doing right now?

When the credits for *Anatomy of a Murder* rolled past, Mike whispered in my ear, "I like all the actors in this movie."

"But it's in black and white," I whispered back.

Mike nodded.

I expected a movie with bright colors, like *Pillow Talk* that Carolyn and I had seen one Sunday afternoon.

The strange, jazzy piano music was discordant and the movie seemed to be about fishing, of all things.

I shifted in my seat and glanced at Mike.

Then Lee Remick appeared on the screen and a murmur went through the audience. She was beautiful, but her clothes were so tight they could have been painted on. She wanted Jimmy Stewart, who played the part of a lawyer, to defend her husband. He was in jail for killing a man who had supposedly raped her.

At the word *rape*, a shocked gasp came from the audience. I kept my eyes on the screen. I'd never heard that word used in public.

Had Mike known this movie was so . . . *frank*?

When Lee Remick told Jimmy Stewart what she wore underneath her clothes—a slip, panties, and a bra—I felt the heat of embarrassment radiating off Mike.

When we left the movie theater, snow was falling again. The adult complications of the movie still gripped me as our shoes pressed gray prints into the slush that muted the sounds of traffic.

"Jimmy Stewart was good," I said. "I liked the courtroom scene."

"Yeah."

"And Lee Remick was awfully pretty." I wanted to get that part out in the open and let Mike know it was okay that he had taken me to a movie like that. But Daddy better not find out.

"Yeah." Mike's face colored as he helped me into the car. "I didn't know they made movies so"—he struggled for the right word—"so plainspoken."

"Me neither."

On the edge of town, we had to wait for a train to pass on the tracks.

Mike rolled down his window, letting a few fat flakes of snow drift in. "I like the sound of trains," he said.

The hiss of the brakes and clanging of the cars made an odd kind of music—sort of like the jazz in the movie.

"Why?"

"It's a rhythm for going someplace. Like you have a rhythm for dancing or a rhythm for mowing."

The train eased along slowly, almost stopped. People read or looked out the window, cozy in their warm pods. A soldier slept, his seat reclined. The dark plush seatbacks were covered with white linen.

When the dining car inched into view, I pointed. "Look!"

A woman in a red hat nodded as the man across from her poured something from a silver pot. White-coated waiters moved around with silver trays. Flowers sprung from vases on each table.

"Can you believe it?" I breathed.

Mike smiled. "It's almost as good as a movie."

"Where do you suppose they're going?"

"Chicago, probably," Mike said, "since it's a north-bound train. From there, who knows?"

I shivered. Chicago. I could barely believe it.

Mike rolled up the window as the train gathered speed.

"I'm going into the air force after high school," he said as the caboose came into view.

"The air force? Why?"

"The service is a good way to get an education. To see the world."

"I'd like to see the world too," I said. Actually, I'd

be content to see a college campus. And there was one just sixty miles down the road.

"Hey, maybe we could see it together," Mike said, glancing at me with a smile.

"Yeah, I could disguise myself as a boy and join up with you." That was probably the only way I was going to get out of this place.

Mike reached across the seat for my hand. "If the whole world thought we were boys, then we could be together all the time," he said.

"Exactly." I'd like that. "I'd just cut my hair a little shorter."

"You could wear my clothes. They'd be loose, but that would be good."

"I could roll up the pant legs and talk in a deep voice," I said, going down an octave.

I shut my eyes. It was like something out of Shakespeare. The young couple roaming the world together, everybody assuming we were just good friends. Only we would know the truth. What freedom we would have.

When Mike stopped the car in front of my house, he turned my face to his. As we kissed, I caught the slightly salty taste of popcorn on his lips. I ran my fingers along his jaw and let them wander to the magic line where our mouths met. With a sound, Mike grasped my wrist, kissing my fingers, holding my hand to his face, pressing my palm to his lips.

I held my breath with longing and confusion.

Finally, he kissed my palm gently and folded my fingers closed.

"It's okay," he whispered.

I nodded in the darkness.

We walked to the house, our feet in step, his fingers locked between mine. At the door, he cupped my face. His eyes shone in the snow light. He brushed his thumbs lightly outward, shaping a smile on my face.

"Good night," he whispered, not kissing me again, sensing I was on edge.

Who knew when the door might open and Mama might pop out?

I stood in the entryway watching Mike leave. I waited while his car circled through our drive, and then I followed the red dots of his taillights as long as I could see them.

I heard Mama stirring around in the kitchen, so we would have been safe for another kiss, after all.

Little diamonds of melting snow glistened on the sleeves of her coat as I slipped it off.

Chapter 12

On the day before Christmas vacation, Mrs. Ballard told us to close our books and she would tell us a story about a famous seventeenth-century mathematician named Pierre de Fermat.

Mrs. Ballard made the history of mathematics intriguing and sometimes even romantic. I put down my pencil and slid my book away.

"I'll tell you about Fermat's Last Theorem," she said, "and you can think about it over Christmas vacation."

I saw Nate glance at the ceiling, but Bud looked interested.

"Maybe one of you will prove it," Mrs. Ballard suggested, smiling. "Although it's called a theorem, no known proof exists. Fermat just scribbled the theorem in the margin of a book and noted that he had *discovered* a proof, but the margin was too small for him to show it there."

When Mrs. Ballard told us these stories, her brown eyes glowed behind her thick-lensed glasses. Her curly hair caught the light.

"Fermat's proof was never found," she told us. "And for the last three hundred years, mathematicians have been captivated by the problem."

Mrs. Ballard glanced around the room as if it were a great deal bigger than the converted supply room where our tiny class met. Sometimes she made me feel as if it actually was.

"People's lives have been changed by Fermat's Last Theorem," she said. "Take Paul Wolfskehl, for example."

"Never heard of him," Nate muttered.

"Well, he was a man—a very rich man—who was jilted by the woman he loved. Herr Wolfskehl was so heartbroken," Mrs. Ballard went on, "that he decided to kill himself."

"How did he do it?" Nate fought the charm of Mrs. Ballard's storytelling with clinical interest.

I narrowed my eyes at him.

Bud was rapt.

"Well, that's the interesting part," Mrs. Ballard said. "You see, because he was very wealthy and a man of many responsibilities—and very meticulous—he actually scheduled his suicide. He planned to kill himself on the stroke of midnight on a certain day far enough in the future to allow himself to get his affairs in order."

But what did that have to do with Fermat's Last Theorem?

"When the day came to kill himself, all was in order. He'd made his will. Signed the trusts. And he had a few hours to wait before his midnight appointment with death."

Mrs. Ballard fell silent.

What a strange man—to schedule suicide as if it were an appointment with the dentist.

"While he waited in his library," Mrs. Ballard went on, "he wandered to the bookshelf and picked up a volume about the puzzle of Fermat's Last Theorem. He ultimately got so caught up in the puzzle that midnight came and went and he forgot to kill himself."

A good math problem would take a person's mind off everything for a while—though I doubted any math could totally take my mind off Mike.

"And he was so grateful to Fermat's Last Theorem for saving his life that he endowed the Wolfskehl Prize of a hundred thousand marks to whoever finally proves it."

Even Nick's head snapped up. "So what's that worth in our money?"

Mrs. Ballard shrugged. "Who knows anymore? But thousands and thousands of dollars at least."

"Is that money still out there?" Bud asked.

"Indeed it is," Mrs. Ballard said.

I saw the light in Bud's eyes. Thousands of dollars was mind-boggling to anybody, but to Bud—whose family was so poor—it was all the magic in the world and beyond.

"Tell us about this theorem," Bud demanded.

"Well, it looks very simple—which may be one reason so many people have tried to prove it." She turned to the board and wrote the Pythagorean theorem.

$$a^2 + b^2 = c^2$$

"As familiar as your own toothbrush, right?" she asked.

We'd been using that equation since grade school when right triangles were involved. Even Carolyn probably knew the Pythagorean theorem.

Mrs. Ballard wrote:

$$3^2 + 4^2 = 5^2$$
$$9 + 16 = 25$$

"Pythagorean triples, right?" she asked.

We nodded. Those were combinations of whole numbers that perfectly fit the equation.

The only other Pythagorean triple I could call to mind was five, twelve, and thirteen.

There were triples made up of numbers in the thousands that I couldn't remember. But I did remember Mrs. Ballard telling us that the triples became harder and harder to find as the numbers got larger, but that it had been proved that there were an infinite number of them.

Mrs. Ballard wrote another equation on the board just like the first. The only difference was that she changed the exponent from two to three.

$$a^3 + b^3 = c^3$$

"Mathematicians discovered long ago that finding whole-number triples for this equation appears to be impossible," she said.

She erased the cube exponent and replaced it with a four. "Equally impossible."

She changed the four to 789, making the point that the exponent could be infinitely large and hunting for a triple among all those numbers would be hopeless.

"They were pretty sure there were no triples out there," Mrs. Ballard concluded.

"But being pretty sure isn't the same as *proving* it," I blurted out. Finally, I understood the magnitude of Fermat's Last Theorem.

Mrs. Ballard smiled at me.

"So Fermat's Last Theorem says simply that there are no whole-number solutions—other than zero, of course—to the equation if the exponent is greater than two. Mathematicians have always believed that he was right, but no one has ever been able to prove it."

Fascinating. It looked so simple. So tantalizingly easy. No wonder it captivated people.

I glanced at Bud, who was gazing at the board as if he had just opened his best Christmas present—which he probably had.

"If we work on it over vacation, do we get extra credit?" he asked.

Mrs. Ballard looked delighted that Bud wanted to spend part of the holidays on math. "Ten points for some thoughtful work." And then she added, her eyes smiling, "Twenty points for an airtight proof."

"If nobody has proved it in three hundred years, I don't think you're gonna crack it over Christmas, Bud," Nate said.

"Maybe nobody offered extra credit before."

Not to mention thousands and thousands of dollars.

Our Christmas promised to be hard without Meema; perhaps the puzzle of Fermat's Last Theorem could make me forget, just as it had Paul Wolfskehl.

Chapter 13

We always celebrated Christmas with a feast at Meema and Granddad's house on Christmas Day. But this year, things were jumbled up as if, in the confusion, we might not notice Meema's absence.

Instead of ham, Mama prepared rib roast; instead of candied apples, cranberry relish; instead of pecan pie, angel food cake. And we feasted on Christmas Eve instead of Christmas Day.

Despite the lingering aroma of baked sweets and seared meat, and despite our best china and prettiest tablecloth, I couldn't eat.

Granddad looked at his plate, pushed the food around, and finally took several rapid bites, then nodded thanks to Mama. The fireplace popped in the living room, and I could see the reflection of the Christmas tree in the glass face of the dining room clock as the minutes labored past.

I carried dishes into the kitchen, my face stiff with dried tears. I heard Granddad blow his nose with a great honking sound, then mumble "Sorry."

When we were finished with dessert, Daddy poked the fire and threw on another log. "I think everybody should open a present tonight," he announced.

"Mama, Mama!" the twins yelled, spinning through the dining room.

"Daddy says open a present. Right now." In her excitement, Cassie twisted herself up in the long, hanging corner of the tablecloth.

The twins' spinning and giggling cheered us all, and I found myself under the tree shaking the boxes with my name on them, wondering which—if any— could possibly hold the slide rule that I'd put at the top of my Christmas list with a star by it.

The twins ripped open their packages.

I glanced at Granddad sitting on the couch. "Would you open my present to you, Granddad?" I asked, handing it to him.

He nodded and began to slip off the ribbon. His black dress shoes were dusty. Meema would never have let him go out without brushing his shoes.

At Kresge's, I'd bought him a box of three white handkerchiefs with a "C" for Conway embroidered on the corner. Why had I given him handkerchiefs? Although he thanked me as if I'd done the kindest thing in the world, I wished I'd given him something more comforting, like a huge box of chocolate-covered cherries.

The gift I chose to open turned out to be an angora fur collar to wear at the neckline of my sweaters.

"Won't you look pretty!" Mama said when I held it to my throat.

Later, I lay in bed staring out the window, thinking about the dark rectangle that would contain the glow of Mike's window if he still had his light on.

I probably wouldn't see him for a couple of days.

In the living room, my parents were creeping around playing Santa. When Melanie and Cassie got up in the morning, they'd find unwrapped toys that Santa had been carrying around on his sled as he went from house to house, searching for good little boys and girls. There would be something for me too.

A thud came from the living room and I heard Mama make a shushing sound and Daddy laugh.

"Anna, Anna!" One of the twins was pulling on my pajama sleeve. "Santa came! Wake up!"

It was still dark out, but lights from the living room cast a glow down the hall.

"Daddy says we can't see what's under the tree until you're up. We can't even peek around the corner! So hurry!" Cassie tugged my hand and Melanie leapt on the bed and yanked back the covers.

Daddy was warming the backs of his legs in front of the fireplace and Mama was bringing out a plate of rolls from the kitchen. The room smelled of burning hickory, cinnamon, and coffee.

"Look!" Melanie gasped. "Furniture!"

Santa had parked a small table with two little matching folding chairs in front of the tree.

Each of the twins scrambled into a chair. "It's our own table!" Cassie declared.

"Is it for the cave, Mama?" Melanie asked. "Did Santa bring it so we'd have furniture for the cave?"

"Who knows? Maybe."

"I'll bet he brought Anna something too," Daddy said.

I saw an unwrapped gift under the tree, but it surely couldn't be for me. It was a train case. A white Samsonite train case.

Daddy was looking right at it, then wiggling his eyebrows at me.

I picked it up by the handle, turning it this way and that, inspecting the two brass latches, the brass corners. I supposed I could use it when I spent the night at Carolyn's house, but surely it had cost as much as a slide rule. Maybe more.

I struggled to smile. "It's nice." I couldn't believe my parents had spent money on this instead of a slide rule.

Daddy nodded.

We opened our presents, taking turns. Inside my four packages were new pajamas and a robe, a white blouse with roll-up sleeves that Carolyn said was the zenith of fashion, and a light blue sweater with snowflakes around the neck and cuffs. I stacked my empty boxes together, disappointed.

Later, while Mama was fixing breakfast and Cassie and Melanie sat at their new table working on a puzzle, I opened my train case. It had a tray on top, which I lifted out. The inside of the case was lined in an off-white silk, and there were three elasticized pockets—one on each end and one along the back. I slipped my hand inside the back pocket to take out the cardboard sizer.

Daddy was watching me, smiling, taking account of the expression on my face as my fingers discovered the shape of the slide rule.

Out of its plastic case, it smelled faintly industrial, its edges as smooth as soap. The center strip glided back and forth with the ease of silk on silk. The gradients were tiny, but with my glasses they would be perfectly readable.

"Thank you, Santa," I mouthed silently to Daddy. "Thank you, thank you, thank you."

He winked.

At school, I'd use it modestly, letting Bud borrow it. This glorious slide rule would make me feel as chosen and special as any Homecoming Queen.

Chapter 14

The day after Christmas, Mike called.

"I don't have money," he said. "But do you want to go out anyway? Maybe we could just drive around town and look at Christmas decorations."

"Of course I want to go. Let me ask Mama."

"What are you going to do?" she quizzed me as I waited with my hand over the mouthpiece.

"Just drive around to see the Christmas lights."

She hesitated, and I saw the uncertainty on her face. Usually Mike and I went to a movie or a ballgame—something with definite starting and ending times.

"I suppose it would be okay," Mama finally said.

The night was foggy and warm when Mike picked me up. As soon as we were out of the driveway, he slipped a small, slim box from his pocket and laid it in my lap. It was tied with silver ribbon.

Mike and I had already exchanged Christmas gifts. "What's this?"

"Open it," he said.

Inside, something wrapped in white tissue paper lay the length of the box. As I folded back the wrapping, gold shimmered in the lights from the dash.

The bracelet was cool and heavy, smooth except for the engraving of Mike's name. His ID bracelet.

He met my eyes for a second. "Will you wear it?" he asked, pulling to the side of the road, stopping and turning off the lights. We were deep in the country and there might not be a car along for hours.

I drew my fingers along the bracelet, imagining how it would feel on my wrist.

"I love you so much, Anna," Mike said, pressing his face into my hair.

"I love you too," I told him, finding it hard to say the next thing. "But the bracelet might not be a good idea."

"Why not?"

"I think my parents are getting worried—that we're getting too serious. Mama almost didn't let me go out with you tonight."

Mike kissed me, his hand tracing the shape of my body along my shoulder, my breast, my waist, my thigh. I kissed him back, dizzy and not caring. If he wanted me to wear his bracelet I would.

I let him fasten it around my wrist, feeling his fingers trembling.

"Your parents don't need to worry," he said. "But it can be our secret if you want it to. Just wear it when we're alone."

I touched his bracelet on my left wrist, then Meema's on my right. Meema's was light and tinkly. Mike's was heavy and loose.

"It feels strange." I moved my arm around so the bracelet slid and turned on my wrist. "Do your parents know you're giving it to me?"

Mike shook his head.

"Won't they wonder what happened to your bracelet? You wear it every day. Your mom will notice you don't have it on."

"They'll figure it out. They'll put two and two together, mathematician," he teased.

"I'm afraid my folks are putting two and two together," I said.

"You sound like a train," Mike said, brushing my hair behind my ear.

"Seriously, Mike. What if they decide we're too young to be dating—like this?"

He laughed. "Just tell them if they don't let you date me you'll go in your bedroom and do calculus," he said, kissing me again.

I couldn't keep from laughing at what he'd said. Our teeth bumped and I pulled back, smiling.

He was smiling too. "What?" he said.

I shook my head.

Then the lights of a car cresting the hill destroyed our privacy and Mike started the car.

In Baxter, we drove west along Santa Claus Lane. The Rotary Club had set out cedar trees for about ten blocks to the sprawling, hilly city cemetery. Each tree glowed with ropes of colored lights.

We turned around at the cemetery and headed back into town. The moisture in the air made little auras around the colored lights.

"You want to just walk?" Mike asked. "Look in the store windows?"

I nodded.

He drove around the square once and then parked on the north side. Since it was a weeknight, all the stores were closed and the streets almost empty. We saw people sitting in the restaurant of the Hamilton Hotel, mainly salesmen in brown suits smoking cigars.

The ticket seller at the movie theater was looking at a magazine. I noticed an advertisement for a John Wayne Western, which Meema would have liked.

We drifted past the large plate-glass windows of Pharaoh's, which had mannequins in jewel-colored satin dresses, ready for New Year's Eve parties. An enormous globe with mirrored facets revolved slowly over their heads.

I held my right hand cocked back awkwardly to hold Mike's ID bracelet in place.

"I'm afraid I'll lose it," I confessed. "I'm afraid it will fall off my wrist."

Mike took my hand and slid the bracelet down as far as it would go. "You won't lose it," he said. "It's a perfect fit."

Chapter 15

We packed away the Christmas decorations on New Year's Day while the smell of white bean soup—which Mama cooked for good luck—filled the house. I didn't remind her that we'd made white bean soup last year on New Year's Day, and look what had happened to Meema.

"Now," Mama said, sitting down at the dining room table with a steno pad and pen, "we need to get ready for your teacher's visit. Get out the sterling sugar bowl and creamer," she directed, "and the sugar shell and the silver polish."

Under her instruction, I polished our only three pieces of silver. My fingers turned black, plus I had homework to do. Well, maybe not real homework. But I wanted to practice with my slide rule some more so that on Monday I would look casually expert.

"I wonder if Mrs. Myers likes ladyfingers," Mama mused, but didn't wait for a response. "I guess it's not the kind of thing you like or don't like. It's just the kind of thing you serve."

When I got home from school on Monday, the smell of Johnson's Paste Wax almost sent me back out the door. Mama was on her hands and knees in a pair of old slacks, her face flushed. The radio was playing.

"Take your shoes off," she commanded before I was even through the door. "No shoes on the floor until after Mrs. Myers's visit." And she went back to rubbing and swirling an old green towel against the waxed wood, keeping time to "The Battle of New Orleans."

"Anna, do you think you could iron the linen tablecloth and napkins?" she called.

I was changing clothes and tucking away the note somebody—no doubt Carolyn—had slipped between the pages of my geometry book.

Simile for a girl with a slide rule: Long separated by cruel fate, the star-crossed lovers raced across the grassy field toward each other like two freight trains, one having left Chicago at 6:36 p.m. traveling at 55 mph, the other from St. Louis at 4:19 at a speed of 35 mph.

"Anna?" Mama called again.

"Coming."

The twins were sliding down the hall in their stocking feet, crashing to the floor with laughter.

"You girls are going to get splinters in your bottoms," Mama warned. "And I better not see any streak marks in the hall."

The next day after school, when I walked in the door, the twins were starched into submission, wearing their red plaid dresses with white collars and their Mary Janes.

"We can walk on the floor now," Cassie whispered. "But gently." The twins walked single file like old ducks, bringing their heels down softly, then their toes. "See?" Cassie said. "Like that."

"There's Mrs. Myers," Mama said, glancing out the

88

picture window. "Let her in, Anna. But wait until she knocks."

My heart was pounding more than if Mike was coming up the walk. "Come in," I said, forgetting to wait for the knock.

Mrs. Myers's face glowed. "Hello!" she said as if we hadn't seen each other in a long time.

Mama came out of the kitchen looking pretty in her cream-colored silk shirt and bias-plaid skirt and gold earrings.

For a few minutes, Mama and my teacher went around the house, Mrs. Myers asking particularly about the paintings that decorated the walls.

"My husband's mother had painted them," Mama explained.

Eventually, we all sat around the dining room table, which had been polished to a near-blinding sheen. We sipped coffee out of the good china. Mama allowed me to drink coffee because I'd gotten in the habit at Meema's years ago, but she didn't really approve. The twins sat on the other side of the table drinking milk and playing with their ladyfingers.

Mrs. Myers and Mama chatted about Home Ec for a while. Thank God they didn't dwell on sewing.

"We're in a unit now," Mrs. Myers said, "on grooming

and health. Maybe Anna has told you that we've been discussing things like skin care and makeup. Soon we'll be talking about human bodies of both genders and reproductive organs."

Mama shot a look at the oblivious twins.

"We'll be watching a movie in February on child-birth."

Mama turned pale and sat up a little straighter.

"It seems strange, doesn't it? Many parents explain these things to their children at home, but it's part of the school curriculum now. We'll talk about birth control too."

I wanted to crawl under the table. I felt the heat rising. Mama took a deep breath and blotted her lips with one of the linen napkins.

"Specifically we'll be discussing the use of con-doms and the rhythm method," Mrs. Myers went on.

"Oh," Mama breathed.

"Inside of marriage, of course," Mrs. Myers added, her voice conciliatory, implying that *I* didn't need to know this information until some distant point in the future when I found Daddy's mythical man and settled down.

I thought of Christine at church who'd had to get

married. And Marla, a year ahead of me at school, who'd dropped out to get married right before Christmas and was living with her husband's family in Mills City. And the other girls who dropped out every year because they were pregnant.

In the silence, one of the twins belched quietly.

"Excuse me," they said in unison.

Mrs. Myers made herself sound matter-of-fact and teacherlike. "Family planning is a new unit in the school district. And we want to make sure parents know about it. I hope Anna will bring home some of the handouts and let you look at them."

I started breathing again when Mrs. Myers moved on to my report card. My parents would find good grades and praise from my teachers, and she hoped they were thinking about college for me. "If you start planning for it, it's easier financially when the time comes."

I sipped my coffee, my embarrassment settling and gratitude for Mrs. Myers blossoming.

"Has Anna talked to you about participating in the math contest in April?" she asked.

The cup rattled as I set it in the saucer. I thought she would just talk about Home Ec things.

Mama shook her head, looking at me.

"Well, Mr. Carson asked me to mention that particularly. It's at the university, the third Saturday in April. He hopes Anna can go. He'll be taking at least one other student." Mrs. Myers gave me her best smile—the one that showed a deep dimple in her right cheek. "And I think it would be good for Anna."

I wanted to throw my arms around Mrs. Myers's neck and kiss her on both cheeks, hoping that an endorsement from a Home Ec teacher might finally mean something to my parents.

"I'll mention it to my husband," Mama said.

I didn't want to embarrass Mama by saying in front of Mrs. Myers that I had mentioned it to Daddy back in the fall. I'd never thought of talking to Mama about it.

That evening, after Mrs. Myers was gone and while Daddy was changing out of his work clothes, I heard my parents' muffled voices through the closet that separated our rooms. I figured she was telling him what Mrs. Myers had said about the family planning unit or the trip to the university, or both.

As we sat down to supper, I couldn't even wait

until Mama had the twins' plates filled before I began my campaign.

"Mr. Carson was really impressed with the slide rule I got for Christmas, Daddy."

He looked at me, his head to one side, knowing something else was coming.

"Does the slide rule mean you might be thinking about letting me go to the university for the math contest?"

I saw by the arc of his eyebrows that it didn't. Whatever Mama had said, she hadn't convinced him.

"Your slide rule is like your glasses, Anna. I don't want you to have to work too hard at your studies. That's all. You'll be out of high school after next year, and these things won't seem important anymore."

"Did Mama tell you what Mrs. Myers said about college?"

He nodded.

"Well, this would be a chance to visit one."

He dodged my argument. "If you still want to go to college when the time comes, maybe we can work it out." He emphasized the *maybe*.

"Perhaps Anna could be a teacher," Mama jumped in. "Like Mrs. Myers. She could teach Home Economics."

I certainly couldn't see myself trying to show another person how to sew or talking to them about condoms.

"Well, if I ever might go to college—to become a Home Economics teacher and all"—I swallowed the lie and took a breath—"the math contest would be a good chance to have a look at the campus."

Daddy glanced at Mama, and I sensed her tiny nod. *Please.*

He studied my face as if trying to assess the damage of too many axioms. "All right," he finally said.

I jumped up and kissed his cheek. "Thank you!"

He shook his head.

Later, I sat at my desk looking at the three watercolors that Mike had done. He'd recently bought a set of watercolor paints, and I'd given him a little book on watercolor painting for Christmas.

Maybe he would like to be an artist when he was older. But I could hear his parents telling him to go in the air force or get a job at the factory where his dad worked.

I stared across the snow-dusted field at the light in Mike's window, wishing he could know how happy I was that I was going to visit the university.

Part 3 : Spring

The mathematician's patterns, like the painter's or the poet's, must be beautiful; the ideas, like the colours or the words, must fit together in a harmonious way. Beauty is the first test: there is no permanent place in the world for ugly mathematics.

—G. H. HARDY (1877–1947),
BRITISH MATHEMATICIAN

Chapter 16

The night of the Spring Fling, Mike picked me up at dusk. Lacy white dogwood edged the road.

Mike turned the car into a short lane that quail hunters used and shut off the engine. The last of the sunset turned the sky a blue-orange above the woods.

"Let's park here just for a little while," he said, rolling his window down.

I rolled mine down too. The air was perfectly still.

We sat, Mike on his side of the car and me on mine, our fingers twined in the middle. I'd already pinned on my corsage at home, Mama helping me while Mike showed the twins two carved dolls from Kentucky that his mother had sent over to them. The corsage had fake florist leaves and a tiny silk butterfly with a sprinkle of glitter on its wings.

"You look pretty," Mike said, and I felt his eyes on me just as I had that morning on the bus so long ago when he'd first asked me out.

I had on a sleeveless, pale blue taffeta dress that Mama had made. It was the first thing she'd sewed for me. Meema had made my clothing until she died. So standing in my slip last week while Mama held the pieces of cool taffeta to my skin, shaping and marking, had felt very strange.

"I like the twilight," Mike said.

"You feel like you're being pulled backward and forward at the same time." I watched the sky flare with a last streak of gold. "Like us."

He opened my purse, feeling for the gold links of his bracelet, and reached for my wrist, fastening it on.

When the shadows were almost gone, he got out of the car and walked a few feet back toward the ditch. I heard a rustle and saw a shaking of white dogwood blossoms and in seconds, Mike opened my door and reached for my hand to help me out of the car.

"For you," he said, brushing the sprig of dogwood against my cheek, then putting his arm around my waist and drawing me to him.

He smelled of Aqua Velva. As we kissed, he held me pressed to his body. I raised on my tiptoes, tightening my arms around his neck, wanting to be even closer.

Finally, catching my breath, I captured his hands. "Wait. My dress. Taffeta wrinkles."

"Okay," he whispered, folding my hands behind my back, nuzzling my hair. "Okay."

In the school parking lot, I hung on to Mike's hand for balance as I tiptoed, trying not to skin the heels of my new shoes in the gravel.

"Do you know how to dance?" I asked him.

"Yes. Do you?"

"I've *seen* people dance on *American Bandstand* at Carolyn's house."

Inside, the hallways were dim and quiet. But in the gym, the decorations committee had rigged a spotlight over a small area.

"There's Carolyn and Tom." I waved.

Carolyn had asked Tom to the annual girls-ask-boys dance by sliding a scribbled invitation across to him while the history teacher was listing the Axis powers on the board. Tom had printed *ok* at the bottom and slid it back to her.

The cavernous space of the gym had a coolness that made me wish I'd brought in my sweater.

Mrs. Ballard stepped away from the refreshment table and ran her hands briskly up and down my arms as if she sensed I was cold. The other chaperones were married couples. Mrs. Ballard was the only divorced person I knew.

She steered my shoulders, turning me around slowly, looking at my new dress. Her hands smelled of cookie frosting. "Don't you look pretty!" she said.

Carolyn ran over and hooked her arm through mine. "This is so much fun," she whispered. "Tom's a good dancer."

Tom was right behind her with a peculiar smile on his face, and then I saw up close it was just pink punch stains.

I took Mike's hand. According to etiquette, I had to wait for him to ask me to dance. I squeezed his hand. Somebody had put slow music on the record player. Surely I could manage that.

"Would you like to dance?" he asked.

I felt Carolyn's critical assessment as Mike put his right hand on my waist. Our knees and toes bumped at first, and I swayed off balance. He didn't dance like Carolyn, with whom I'd practiced.

But I relaxed, entrusting myself to him.

"Thank you," he said when the music ended.

I led him toward the refreshment table. "I frosted those." I pointed to sunburst-shaped cookies with white frosting and yellow sprinkles.

Mrs. Ballard put on a new record. "Let's Hokey-Pokey," she called.

Somebody groaned and Carolyn rolled her eyes at me. The Hokey-Pokey was for little kids. But Mike and I crammed the last bits of cookie into our mouths and joined the circle.

When I put my *left arm in* to *shake it all about*, Mike's bracelet swung loosely on my wrist, catching the light.

Later, we danced to "Love Me Tender" and I stepped close to Mike and shut my eyes, laying my cheek against his shoulder.

As we moved around the floor, I noticed Mrs. Ballard standing by the refreshment table, watching us with a wistful look on her face.

"Wouldn't it be awful to have everybody judging you just because you were divorced," I murmured in Mike's ear.

He knew who I was talking about, of course.

"Yeah," he said. "I like Mrs. Ballard."

After the slow dance, Carolyn got them to play "C. C. Rider" and lined us up for the Stroll.

Then one of the chaperones started the Bunny-Hop with prizes for the highest and the silliest hop.

Mike finally took off his sport coat, and Carolyn's naturally curly hair burst out in a frizz.

When parents started turning up about ten o'clock we were doing the Limbo—another one of Mrs. Ballard's ideas. I had long since kicked off my shoes, and would have gone in the bathroom and stripped off my nylons and garter belt if I'd known where to put them.

Outside, the night air was cold against my sweat-damp body. I got in the car and pulled on my sweater.

Tom tapped on the car window. "Do you want to go for a sandwich at the B&B? Carolyn and I are."

Mike looked at me.

"Sure," I said, waving to Carolyn, who was messing with the radio dial in Tom's car. She caught a station and "Kansas City" pounded the air.

Later, we all sat in a booth at the B&B, eating messy barbecue and drinking Cokes. Carolyn flipped through the pages of the little jukebox standard on our table, reading off titles.

Tom handed her a quarter.

"Okay, which three do you want?" Carolyn asked, and without waiting for an answer said, "'Sixteen Candles' for Anna."

"But I'm not sixteen yet," I protested.

"But only six more days," she said.

On the way home, off the highway and into the country, the headlights picked out bits of barely budding green from the fencerows as we moved through the darkness.

Mike stopped the car on the rumbly wooden bridge over Skillet Fork and we got out. He draped his sport jacket over my shoulders, and the whiteness of his shirt stood out in the moonlight. He'd undone his tie, and it hung loose around his neck.

The water whispered and whistled below us. Peepers chimed from the brush along the creek banks, making an eerie celestial sound.

There were cracks between the bridge boards and I didn't want to get a heel stuck, so I clung to Mike's arm, tiptoeing as he guided me to the railing.

The moonlight showed the timbered support of the railroad bridge that crossed the road bridge at almost right angles. It looked beautiful and complex. Maybe I would enjoy figuring out how to build a bridge someday.

Mike and I stood hip to hip at the railing, watching the water. And when Mike turned and kissed me, the moon and the chirring and the mossy smell of the creek got caught up in the taste of his mouth and the pleasure of his hands.

We stood on the bridge for a long time, my eyes closed and my body clinging to his.

"Anna," Mike finally breathed, lifting his lips from mine, "will you? Please?" His heart pounded against me.

I opened my eyes and the stars seemed to whirl.

"Just this," I whispered, wanting him to go on kissing and touching me.

He made a sound of misery and buried his face in my neck.

I stroked the back of his head. "I'm sorry."

"Why won't you?" The breath of his words stirred against my neck.

"I'm not sure it's right," I told him, kissing the top of his head over and over, loving the close smell of his scalp.

He raised his head and clasped my arms. I could see the shine of his eyes in the moonlight. "Is that the only reason?"

"What if . . ." What if we got caught? I couldn't do that to my family. I had a vision of Christine from church and the humiliation of her family.

"What if you got pregnant?" Mike said. "I won't let that happen." He pulled a small white package out of his pants pocket. "I won't. I promise."

I leaned against his chest, feeling the tears coming. Saying *no* was so hard, but I couldn't say anything else.

Chapter 17

On Sunday morning, when Daddy stopped the car in the Dillons' drive, I felt more self-conscious than I had when Mike and I first started going together. I'd invited him to come to church with me, but it suddenly felt so grown-up. So public. So . . . *sanctioned.*

I waved to him as he came out the back door. He probably felt even more awkward than I did; he was the one who had to ride in the car with my entire family.

Daddy sounded too jovial. "Get in, Mike. Get in!"

"Scoot over!" I whispered to Cassie. But she had turned to stone in the middle of the seat.

"Hello," Mike said, greeting the car at large.

"Beautiful morning," Mama sang. "Scoot over, girls." She made a shooing motion over the back of the seat with her hand.

Melanie and Cassie scrambled to the other side, bumping each other, getting tangled in their skirts.

"Put your legs down!" Melanie scolded Cassie.

I slid to the middle of the back seat, over the transmission hump.

In the church parking lot, I felt people looking.

Inside, I led Mike to the young people's section where Mary Anderson fixed her eyes on him as I unbuttoned my new spring jacket.

Mary peered around me at Mike. "Hi. It's real nice you could come," she said, smiling. "Anna has never invited a boy to church before."

"Well, I'm sure glad it was me," Mike said after a beat.

I felt my neck turn pink.

Later, in Sunday school class, our teacher asked me to introduce my friend, and I did—feeling like part of an official pair instead of just plain Anna Conway.

When we were finishing the lesson from First Corinthians, Mike read before me. "When I was a child, I spake as a child, I understood as a child, I thought as a child: but when I became a man, I put away childish things."

Mike read the words as if they were unfamiliar, as if he were touching them one by one—looking at them from all sides and for the first time.

I'd heard that passage a thousand times, but when Mike read it like that I felt the literalness of it. *Did* people have to put away childish things? Did the twins have to stop believing they would move into their cave this summer with their table and chairs from Santa, the everyday silverware, and all their stuffed animals?

"Anna?" the teacher prompted.

I cleared my throat and touched my glasses, settling them on my face. "For now we see through a glass, darkly; . . . but then shall I know even as also I am known."

"And what do you think that means?" the teacher asked.

But then shall I know even as also I am known could have to do with Mike and me. Not sexually, exactly, but intimately. And I said a prayer that this wasn't sacrilegious. But God really had created me. And Mike. And our feelings. Why would He have created them if they were wrong?

The summer when I was ten and all the other kids were getting baptized, I'd gone forward and said I wanted to accept Jesus Christ as my personal savior and be baptized in Charley Mahood's pond at the end of revival. Then the next day, when the preacher came to call and explained about how the old sinful me would die in the pond, I got scared. I hadn't wanted any part of me to die—not even the sinful part.

"Don't think about it," Meema had advised after the preacher left, drying my tears in her kitchen among the bittersweet—trying to get me to drink some lemonade. "It's just words. Just the way we try to explain things too amazing to understand. And the words make it more scary than it ought to be."

Meanwhile, our Sunday school teacher was still waiting for my answer. What did the Bible mean, *But then shall I know even as also I am known*?

And I gave the standard, approved answer. "I guess it means when we get to heaven, everything will become clear."

The teacher nodded and moved on to read the final verse himself. "And now abideth faith, hope, charity, these three; but the greatest of these *is* charity."

Which everybody knew meant *love*.

When we were leaving, the preacher shook Mike's

hand and welcomed him. Mike smiled and nodded at the preacher's encouragement to come back and bring his family. In the car, the twins, who were getting used to Mike in our Sunday-morning midst, asked if he was coming to our house for dinner.

"We'd love to have you, Mike," Mama said, turning to smile at him over the seat back.

Daddy slowed the car, waiting to see if he should continue straight down the road to Mike's or turn left to our house.

I tried to keep the frown off my face. We weren't married *yet*.

Mike glanced at me. "I think my dad's cousin Ray is driving over from Mills City. But thanks. I'd like to come sometime."

I smiled. Mike was mine, and I wanted people to know that. But I didn't want them to assume so much.

I could easily imagine the trajectory of Christine's life.

I tried to see myself in fifty years, sitting in the front row to hear the preacher better, with my children, grandchildren, and great-grandchildren sprinkled through the congregation behind me.

But I just couldn't. At least not right now.

Chapter 18

The morning of April 6, my sixteenth birthday, I went out the door to catch the bus and there stood Mike, leaning on the banister of the front porch.

"You startled me," I said, catching my breath.

It had turned chilly again in the night, and the edges of the yard were dusted with frost. The early sun made long shadows of the fence posts. Mike had on a heavy flannel shirt over a regular shirt, and the edges of his ears were pink with cold.

"Happy birthday," he said, holding out a giant bouquet of flowering crab apples.

I laughed at the sheer size of it.

Tight rosy buds were scattered among open white

blossoms. The gray branches, punctuated by unfurled leaves, were streaked black from melted frost.

"It's the world's largest bouquet," he announced.

I'd had a vase of crab apple blooms like this in my room at Meema and Granddad's house every spring. Meema had loved this time of year too.

"Don't you like it?" Mike asked.

I smiled. "It's just what I wanted."

"Really?"

"Really." I could hear the bus coming from the north. "Let me give them to Mama to put in water," I said. "Tell Mr. Walters I'll be a minute."

Mike took my armload of books, and I took the large bouquet, having trouble getting it through the door.

"Mama," I called.

She stepped out of the kitchen, still in her housecoat. "I thought you'd gone," she said. "Don't I hear the bus? What's that?" she asked, focusing on the flowers.

"Mike brought them," I explained. "Could you put them in water? I need to hurry."

I ran down the drive. The bus had just stopped, and I saw Mike talking to Mr. Walters, gesturing to me. I bounded up the steps and Mike and I took our usual seat.

At school, as I hung my sweater in my locker, Carolyn thrust a small package tied with curly ribbon into my hands. "Open it, open it," she urged.

Inside, on a square of cotton, lay a pair of earrings—thin disks of brass, about two inches in diameter, enameled in black and green. They made me think of dark, veiled women dancing with castanets.

"I got them at Kresge's! Aren't they gorgeous?"

I turned them in my fingers. "Gorgeous," I said. "Thank you."

In trig class, Bud, who—like me—was nearly wild with excitement about going to the college on April 16 for the math contest, told everybody it was my sixteenth birthday. Mr. Carson burst into "Happy Birthday" and the guys joined in, looking a little embarrassed.

Nate remarked to the world at large, "Anna's sweet sixteen, but I'll bet she's already been kissed."

"And I'll bet Nate hasn't," I said, looking guilelessly heavenward.

When I got home from school, I showed the earrings to Mama, who tried them on, turning her head from side to side like a movie star.

Granddad came for birthday cake after supper, bringing me three stems of Lenten Rose from

Meema's flowerbed. I put them in a small vase and set them on the table. The blooms dropped their faces shyly, as if too wonderful to be seen, showing only their dusty pink undersides and the ruffles of green around their necks.

The Lenten Roses invoked Meema so much that I wondered if she knew what we were doing—celebrating my sixteenth birthday—and if she felt sad or happy, and what she would think of the crab apple blossoms from Mike opening up on my desk.

Chapter 19

$\mathcal{I}$ wore the earrings to church Palm Sunday.

I always cried on that day, wiping the tears away casually, hoping nobody noticed. As we waved palm fronds and sang about Jesus' joyful entrance into Jerusalem, I was torn by knowing how it would all end in a few days. Jesus betrayed—nailed on a cross, writhing in agony.

That afternoon, Mike and I went for a drive. The past few days had been so unseasonably warm that the twins were running around the yard barefoot when Mike and I left. We had the car windows open and the world had a sweet, heavy warmth.

As we drove down a narrow township road, Mike asked me why I'd cried in church.

"I hate the way it ends," I told him. "You know. Good Friday."

The bushes along the roadside were leafing out little paintbrushes of clear, pale green. Mike pulled over and parked.

An abandoned oil rig in the middle of a field and somebody's rusted barbed-wire fence were the only signs of people.

Mike reached across the seat for my hand. "Come here."

I slid across and wrapped my arm around him. "Let's take a walk," I said. "See the Easter flowers over there? We can pick some."

Mike leapt over the ditch and then held his hand out for me, but I still got mud on the heel of my shoe. The ground was smooth underfoot as if the field had never been plowed.

"There was a house here once," Mike said. "Look." He pointed to the remnants of foundation stone half hidden in the greening grass.

He brushed away debris from the old threshold and we sat side by side, knees bent. The Easter flowers bloomed in clumps on either side of us. I picked three and smelled them, then held them to Mike's face.

"I wonder if the people who planted the flowers ever sat here on a Sunday afternoon?" he said after a while.

"Granddad might know. Maybe they went to our church." As an afterthought, I asked Mike why his folks never came. Not that I cared, but everybody else I knew went to church.

"They're not church types. Dad works hard all week and wants a day to rest. Mom would be embarrassed to come without him."

"My family has probably gone to church every Sunday since about the fourth century," I told him, handing him the flowers and trying to wipe the mud off my heel with a clump of grass.

Mike stretched out on the sun-baked foundation stone and put his head in my lap, his face to the sun. In his hands folded across his chest, he held the daffodils. His face glowed pink in the warmth of the day, his eyelids twitched now and then, and his stomach rose with his breath.

"Do you have faith?" I asked him, glad his eyes were shut.

He didn't answer for so long I wondered if he'd dozed off or if I'd really asked the question out loud.

"Yeah," he finally answered. "Do you?"

"Sometimes. Sometimes it's hard to sort out faith from other stuff."

"Faith from church, you mean?" Mike cut straight to what I meant.

I nodded, then realized he couldn't see me because his eyes were still shut. I slipped my hand in between his and the daffodils. He squeezed my fingers and I knew it took discipline for him to lie there, patient with my examination of conscience.

"Faith seems so instinctive. Like eating or breathing. I lost it for a while after Meema died. It was kind of like losing my appetite. But it's coming back."

"Good," Mike said, playing with my fingers. Two of the daffodils had tumbled into the grass. One still lay on his stomach.

I shifted my position, raising Mike's head, and I kissed him, our mouths at funny right angles, which was odd and exciting. I heard Mike groan as he sat up and I was sorry for what I'd done.

"Anna," he said.

"It's wrong."

But was it really wrong?

I buried my face in his neck, hugging him tight.

"No," I said, my voice muffled. Nice girls said *no*. It was their job. It was what boys counted on them to do. A deed done could never be undone. One minus one equaled zero.

Mike kept holding me tight, and I could feel his heartbeat gradually slowing.

"Do you think it's really a sin?" I asked.

"Not compared to killing people or doing something to hurt somebody," he said. "Maybe it's just a little sin."

Chapter 20

The next Saturday morning on the way to the college, we passed through a couple of towns with courthouses on the squares, and most of the stores still closed. Bud and Mr. Carson talked about quail hunting. I watched the countryside go by. Barns, silos, brown earth, white-faced cows, fences. Barns, silos, brown earth . . .

When we got to Markville, I peered out the windows. Was that huge gray stone building the college?

No, that was the First Methodist Church.

Mr. Carson turned left. "Old Main, straight ahead," he announced.

I leaned forward. A castlelike building loomed at the end of the street, about five blocks away. A square tower penetrated the canopy of barely leafed trees.

"I had many classes there," Mr. Carson said, meeting my eyes in the rearview mirror. "Everybody does their freshman year." A few blocks later, he slowed almost to a stop and pointed to the right. "That's the girls' dorm, Anna. And the new Home Ec building across the street."

My head pivoted from side to side as Mr. Carson pointed. "I worked for room and board when I was here," he told Bud. "And I had a weekend job off campus to pay for books and tuition. So it took me a little longer than four years to finish, but not much. I paid for it all myself. It can be done."

Bud nodded. He probably wanted to come here as much as I did.

We turned right in front of Old Main and parked in a sea of cars and buses, then followed drifts of boys into a modern, low-lying building that still smelled of paint. Blond wood caught the sunlight. A bank of registration tables spread along the wall between two sets of double doors. I saw one other girl in the crowd.

"I'll meet you by that painting over there when you're done." Mr. Carson pointed to a huge canvas of surf crashing against rocks.

Bud and I registered by our school, then our names, and we were each handed a card with a number on it.

Inside the auditorium, alternating rows of aqua and orange seats dropped down in an amphitheater shape. Our entire high school, including all the teachers, bus drivers, janitors, and secretaries—times four—could fit in here.

I clutched my card with the number D6.

"Bye," Bud said, flashing his number of J22.

I went down the steps to Row D. Seat 6 was a perfect number according to Mrs. Ballard. Its factors—three, two, and one—added up to itself.

Why didn't I have a little desk like the other students?

Then I saw a boy two rows ahead lift something up from the side of his chair and a paddle-shaped desk folded across his lap.

I groped beside me and smiled as I slid my own desk into place.

Down front, eight proctors stood in a row, like sentinels guarding the stacks of booklets. I'd been so thrilled about visiting the campus that I hadn't really thought about having to take a test.

As the second hand marked nine on the clock at the front of the room, a proctor explained that we shouldn't put our names on the test booklet or our blue books—just our seat numbers.

What were *blue books*? But then, somebody from the back of the room asked and the proctor explained that we'd record our actual answers in the test booklets, but show our work in a separate place. And he held up a little booklet with a pale blue cover.

I rubbed my suddenly damp hands against my skirt, then put on my glasses and got out my pencils and slide rule. When one of the men laid a test booklet and a blue book in front of me, I printed D6 on the covers.

Many of the problems had a familiar feel—speeding trains and passing cars, simplifying equations and solving for x, calculating areas and volumes.

Sometimes I found myself staring out a window cut high in the wall through which I could see only a little piece of blue sky.

I was asked to figure the width of the stream from C to AB when AB was a line 745 feet long on one bank of the stream, and C was a point on the opposite bank. A equaled 50 degrees 20 seconds and B equaled 51 degrees 30 seconds. This wasn't tough once I got the picture drawn.

Then there was a quadratic equation. For a few of the problems, I tried to use some of the self-taught calculus that I'd dug out of the book Mr. Carson loaned me.

By the time I raised my hand to get another blue book, I felt as if the math crevasse of my brain had opened up and swallowed all my blood and oxygen. I could hardly wait to get out into the sunshine and see the place.

I scribbled D6 on the front and began plotting the graph of a secant function on the graph paper that was folded into the back of the booklets. The narrow, pendulous droop of the graph made me think of a cow's udder.

What was Daddy doing now? What were Mama and the twins doing? What was Mike doing?

I turned around to see if Bud had finished, but he was still there, bent over his desk, his eraser pressed to his forehead as if he were trying to pop the solutions out.

I did the last two problems, then reviewed some of my earlier answers, since I wanted to wait for Bud anyway.

But soon a proctor came to stand beside me. "Time," he said, holding out his hand.

Thank goodness. I handed him the blue books and test booklet.

My left foot had gone to sleep, so I sort of hobbled

up the steps behind Bud. In the lobby, a few people were still around. A man sat at one of the registration tables, smoking and sorting booklets.

The test was over. Now I would get to see the campus.

As we headed for a place called the Student Union for lunch, Bud tried to do a postmortem on a couple of problems with me, but I said no.

I didn't mind the long lunch line because, as we inched along, I got a good look at the bookstore, the bursar's office—which Mr. Carson said meant the office where you paid your college bills—a room where some college guys were shooting pool, a lounge where people clustered around a television set, and—finally—the dining room.

Today the room overflowed with high school kids, gawking like Bud and me. But I saw a few real college students, studying or reading as they ate.

"I'll have a chili dog," Bud told the person behind the counter.

I hadn't been thinking about what to order, so I asked for the same thing—then regretted it a few minutes later when the sandwich oozed orange all over my hands and probably my face.

I gobbled it down and scrubbed at my mouth with a napkin.

"I'm done," I announced.

Mr. Carson laughed. "We have plenty of time, Anna. The awards ceremony isn't until three o'clock."

Chapter 21

We strolled by Old Main again. Narrow, leaded windows reflected the sky. A broad flight of stairs led up to the second-story entrance. I could practically feel the worn granite beneath my feet.

A girl came down the steps. She had on a cotton shirtwaist and flats, much like me. She carried a few books. She could be going to the girls' dorm, or shopping, or for a walk, or to meet her boyfriend.

I could be her. I could be here.

"That's the music building." Mr. Carson pointed. "That's where we'll go for the awards ceremony at three."

"It looks like a princess should live in the tower," I

said, "with a dragon guarding her." It was even more castlelike than Old Main—golden brick, with turrets, and stone-faced archways. The sounds of someone playing a piano floated down from an open third-story window.

"Maybe it's the princess," Bud whispered, nudging me.

Around the corner, a fountain trickled water into a mossy mosaic pool. A few tiny chartreuse leaves floated on the top.

"Look at all those pennies," Bud said.

"People toss them in and make a wish," Mr. Carson explained, reaching in his pocket and sending a penny splashing into the pool.

Bud copied him.

I shut my eyes and wished Daddy would let me come here someday. But I didn't throw away a perfectly good penny.

We walked north, through a new part of the campus. Low, streamlined buildings had raw landscaping with thin whiskers of grass just emerging.

"None of this was here when I was. We had our math and science classes in barracks left over from World War II." Mr. Carson made a broad motion. "All this has popped up overnight. There's so much money being put into science and math education now. We've got to catch up with the Russians."

"Or learn the Cyrillic alphabet," Bud said, "and how to order a chili dog in Russian."

We strolled through the new part of the campus. *Hancock Physics Building. Cassiday Center for the Sciences. Landis Memorial Mathematics Building.*

Mr. Carson suggested we go have a look at Miller Hall, the girls' dorm. As we doubled back across the campus, I saw couples walking together. I would tell Mike what Mr. Carson said about how you could work your way through college. Maybe he didn't really want to go into the air force.

As we entered the main door of Miller Hall, Mr. Carson said, "I dated a girl who lived here. Matter of fact, I married her." And then he blushed as Bud and I glanced at each other.

"So I know a little about the dorm," he explained, clearing his throat. "That's the head resident's office on the left. And on the right are the mailboxes and switchboard."

Windowed mailboxes with combination dials covered a wall. Behind a window, a girl a little older than me moved plugs around in a switchboard. She smiled at us.

"There's the formal lounge," Mr. Carson said. "The guys have to have on coats and ties to go in there and the girls have to be dressed up too."

The room had thick-looking wall-to-wall carpet, heavy draperies, and paintings in gilt frames. Bud's eyes were wide.

"And up the stairs," Mr. Carson said, pointing, "is off-limits to guys. That's where the girls' rooms are."

A glass divider set off the stairs, and HOURS was lettered on the glass.

"What does that mean? 'Ten o'clock Sunday through Thursday, midnight Friday and Saturday'?" I asked.

"It means you have to be in the dorm by those times," Mr. Carson explained.

I would remember that when I talked to Daddy.

We went through the main entry and exited on the other side, going down a flight of stairs and coming out in a three-sided courtyard.

A girl in sunglasses sat on one of the sandstone steps. She had on a pretty, red jumper. Mama would have to make me clothes if I came here.

I tried to imagine myself away from my family, deciding on my own how my days unfolded.

"We'd better get back," Mr. Carson said, pointing up the hill toward the music building.

"Do we have to?" I asked. I wanted to see the library, which looked about twenty times the size of the Baxter courthouse.

"It would be rude not to, Anna," Mr. Carson said. "It's part of the official program."

"Somebody has to clap for the winners," Bud said.

The auditorium looked like pictures I'd seen of old opera houses. Wine-colored velvet seats sloped down toward the stage in tiers. A vast, ornate balcony with gilt and murals hung over our heads.

Because we were almost late, we had to go way down in front to find seats. A man at the podium was just beginning some announcements about how many schools and how many students had participated in the day. I paid attention, but was wishing I could have spent more time touring the campus.

Then another man took the podium and began naming a long list of students who had earned honorable mentions on the test.

Bud and I twisted around to look at who was standing up and hurrying to the stage. I clapped with the rest of the audience as we gave the twenty boys a standing ovation.

The third-place winner was from Mike's old high school. I tried to remember his name to ask Mike if he knew him. As he came forward, his classmates and teachers stood, whistling and whooping.

In the silence, the announcer called the name of the second-place winner and his school went wild too, pounding the seat backs. We all rose to our feet, applauding.

How those boys must feel! Tears came to my eyes.

"Geez, Anna, it's just a math contest," Bud teased, elbowing me.

Tonight I'd try to describe to my parents all that I'd seen. If I could bring it alive to them, maybe they would come with me for a visit.

"Anna Conway."

Bud was looking at me as if I'd turned into a burning bush.

"First place."

Time stopped.

"Anna Conway?" The announcer kept sweeping his gaze over the auditorium.

My brain couldn't get through to my body.

"Have I said that name right? *Anna?*"

Mr. Carson reached out his hand, finally, and pulled me to the aisle. The trip to the stage seemed endless.

I stood at the head of the line as we took our last round of applause. I found Mr. Carson and Bud in the crowd. Bud was jumping up and down and waving, and I waved back. Mr. Carson had the same expression Daddy had after the twins were born.

Chapter 22

"We'll stop here!" Mr. Carson announced, hitting his brakes and wheeling right into the A & W parking lot, sending Bud sliding across the front seat. The car behind us honked.

Inside, Mr. Carson, with a broad gesture toward the menu on the wall, announced, "You can have anything you want, Anna. Anything. You too, Bud. My treat!"

I couldn't possibly eat. But I couldn't say no—not when Mr. Carson was sitting across the booth looking at me like that.

Bud suggested I order a king-sized banana split. "Think of it as queen-sized."

I saw the hunger in his eyes for chocolate, strawberry, and vanilla ice cream—for strawberry, pineapple, and chocolate syrup—for whipped cream, nuts, and maraschino cherries just like in the picture.

"Will you have one too?"

He nodded.

Could I really have won first place? The freckle-faced kids braking their bikes in front of the walk-up window looked real, as did the puddles of moisture around the glasses of ice water on our table. So I must have.

Mr. Carson was still smiling when we eventually pulled into the high school parking lot thirty minutes late. As he followed me to our car, I thought he might burst right through his clothes. He began at the beginning, telling Mama the details of how long the exam was and what we ate for lunch. I saw her fidgeting with the keys, probably worrying what the twins were up to at home.

"And when all the winners were up on the stage except the first-place winner—" Mr. Carson paused for effect.

If only Mama and Daddy could have been in the audience—could have seen all the people.

"—they called *Anna Conway.*"

Mama jerked around to look at me. "Anna?"

Mr. Carson nodded. "That very girl right there."

"Well!" Mama smiled. "Well, my goodness, Anna!"

I could tell on the drive home that she was pleased and excited by the way she kept asking me this and that—had we had any trouble finding the building? Were the questions on the test just like the questions in my math books? Had a dollar been enough for lunch? What had I ordered at the A & W?

I wanted to explain the wonder of being almost the only girl in a sea of boys. But that would make my parents even more reluctant. I wanted to describe the earnestness of the contestants and the admiration of the applause. But that would make me sound like I was bragging.

And despite my grand adventure, the world was just like I'd left it this morning. Bridge boards still rumbled under our tires as we crossed Skillet Fork, and quail still scurried along the edge of the road, running for cover as we approached.

In front of the Dillons' place, Mike worked on a bank, raking out winter kill.

Mama waved at him.

"Let me walk from here," I said. "I'll just talk to Mike a minute and be on home."

She stopped the car and I got out. "Supper won't be long," she called before I shut the door.

Mike leaned against the wooden handle of the rake, his face flushed and his white T-shirt stained where he'd wiped his hands. "Hey," he said. "How was the trip? Was the campus nice?"

"I won," I said.

Mike looked at me, taking time for my words to settle in. We'd never even talked about the contest. "Won? The contest?"

"Yep."

"Hey!" He dropped the rake and clasped my fingers. "Hey!" He danced me around in the road, then he hugged me. He pushed me back and danced me around in the road some more. "Anna won!" he yelled so loudly that all the cows in the countryside probably raised their heads from their grazing.

"Shhhh," I said. But then I just smiled, letting all my pride come out. "I did."

Mike pulled off his dirty T-shirt and spread it on the bank for me. "Tell me everything," he commanded, flopping onto the bank.

I sat beside him.

"Well—" What was there to tell? I had never seen Mike without his shirt before. His skin was smooth. If I touched it, it would feel like warm satin. He didn't have masses of curly hair like Daddy. Just planes and curves of skin, darker than mine, more olive.

"Well—" I took a breath and started again. "It was just a math test, not really very hard. But Mike, you should see the college. It's huge." I described everything, beginning with the Methodist church, which I'd first thought was the college.

I put my hands to the sides of my head and shut my eyes, smiling. The space inside my head was different now. The exponent of my life was bigger.

Mike asked a lot of questions, which slowed down my telling. Not until somebody went by in a truck and waved did I notice how long the shadows had grown.

I jumped up. "Mama said to just stay a minute. I'll be late for supper."

Mike stood up too, but I could tell by the way he stretched out his arm, not letting go of my hand, that he didn't want me to leave. "Let's take a walk later. And you can finish telling me about your day."

"But it will be dark." It would be almost dark by the time I walked the fifteen minutes home for supper.

"I mean really later," he said, waiting for me to understand. I wanted to look away, but he held my eyes. "After supper and after everybody's gone to bed."

How many nights had I stared out my bedroom window at the light in his bedroom window?

Why had God put such a tiny space between us?

I nodded.

Mike knew what I was promising. His face reflected the sunset. "I'll wait at the end of your drive. Come whenever you can after eleven-thirty."

A bit later, when my family was sitting down for supper, Daddy ruffled my hair. "What you did today was real good," he said.

Mike and I would be in so much trouble if we got caught sneaking out.

"Anna won," Melanie announced to the world in general, having no idea what I'd won. And Cassie gave me a hug.

"Since tomorrow is Easter, we're having ham," Mama said. "But next Sunday, I'll make a dinner of all your favorite foods, and we can invite Mike."

I smiled.

My parents trusted me and I was about to betray them.

Chapter 23

The gravel beneath my feet sounded like an avalanche that would bring Daddy running. But my guilty heart was just making everything seem louder. And I'd heard Daddy snoring and Mama emitting those little sounds of contentment that she makes in her sleep.

"Anna." Mike's voice was soft, so much a part of the night and the faint breeze that I wasn't even sure he'd spoken.

He took hold of my hand. "I was afraid you wouldn't come," he whispered, his lips to my ear.

I stepped into the curve of his arm, feeling his ribs through his flannel shirt, smelling the familiar soap smell.

He let me go, but held on to my hand, and we began walking slowly up the road. After my eyes got used to the dark, the little bits of dirt at the edge of the oiled surface glowed palely and marked our path.

There were a handful of weak stars, but no moon. The air had the close feel of changing weather.

"We're off the map," Mike murmured, squeezing my fingers.

"What do you mean?"

"We're not where the world expects us to be— where we've ever been before."

I couldn't tell if we'd walked a half mile from the house or were barely to the edge of the yard line to the north. All I could see were the faint lines at the edge of the road and Mike's shape in the darkness.

"Are you afraid?" Mike said, curling his fingers around my wrists.

His breath was warm against the side of my face.

"Yes. Aren't you?"

I think he smiled. "I guess. But I won't let anything happen, Anna. Don't worry."

"I know."

And I did know that Mike would protect me. And he would never tell.

We began to walk again. I turned up the collar of my long-sleeved shirt.

"Are you cold?" he asked.

"No. Mike, what if a car comes along?"

"You mean now?"

I explained the obvious. "We're walking down the middle of the road at midnight."

"We'll see the car lights coming from way off."

"But what will we *do* if we see the lights coming from way off?"

"I'll show you in a minute," he said. "Come on."

After a few hundred yards, he guided me to the right. "See that big old hickory?"

Even in the darkness, I could make out the tall tree. There was a short little lane by that tree where Daddy sometimes parked farm equipment.

"Here," Mike said. "Let me guide you. Careful, there's a ditch."

But he was too late. I'd stumbled and he had to catch me, yanking me to my feet. And then he was holding me so close.

"Be careful, Anna," he said, his voice shaky. "Walk really close to me."

We found the blanket he'd left rolled up at the base

of the tree, and we shook it out and spread it on the grass.

I had never lain beside Mike before, and his body felt long and narrow. I twined my legs between his, stretching into his kiss. The night was so dark and thick that after a while I couldn't tell where my body ended and Mike's began.

Chapter 24

At school on Monday, Mr. Carson spread the word around. I saw him outside the door of the teachers' lounge talking to Mrs. Ballard, his arms waving like they did when he was excited.

Mrs. Myers gave me a hug in Home Ec. "I'm so glad your parents let you go, Anna. You've made the school proud."

The principal saw me at the water fountain and came up to shake my hand. "We'll remember this on Honors Day," he said. "Maybe you should apply for a scholarship for college, Anna."

By the lockers, Carolyn held my arm up like I'd knocked out Einstein in the first round. "Anna Conway," she boomed. "The winner!"

Kids in the hall shook their heads and smiled.

I snatched back my arm. So much had changed in my life since last Friday. Carolyn knew only a tiny part of it. But it wasn't the kind of thing I could talk to anybody about, not even Carolyn.

Would I have even talked to Meema?

I'd talked to God, who seemed to be listening again. I asked for forgiveness, if it was wrong. And I asked that I wouldn't hurt anybody who loved me. In my mind, I saw the faces of Christine's family as the rumors grew. And I prayed that wouldn't happen to my family.

I told God I couldn't survive that—bringing down shame on my parents.

Mike had been no different than usual on the bus this morning except for what I saw in his eyes. Worry for my worry.

When he'd kissed me good night on Saturday night, stroking my hair, he'd asked if I was okay. I was okay, but I needed time to think. To get used to what had changed.

Mrs. Ballard motioned me to stay after geometry class, and I wanted to thank her anyway, for being such a good teacher. She wasn't like Mr. Carson, who taught us practical things—how to solve problems with algebra, trig, and calculus—things I needed to do well at the math contest. Things I'd need to know to design a bridge or build a dam.

Mrs. Ballard did teach us geometry, of course, with its postulates and proofs and logic. But she went further than that when she talked about pure mathematics—numbers for their own sake beyond any practical application of them—the infinity-times-two capacity of Hilbert's Hotel; the five-pointed star of the Pythagoreans that revealed the Golden Ratio; the mysterious relationship between the numbers in the Fibonacci sequence; prime numbers; perfect numbers; friendly numbers.

"Congratulations, Anna," she said, smiling.

"Thank you. I wouldn't do well without good teachers." And it suddenly occurred to me that Mrs. Ballard had never encouraged me to participate in the math contest.

"You're a special girl," she said. She was looking at me with her arms crossed, holding the textbook, her grade book with our folded homework spraying out of it against her chest. "What's next?"

The blackboard was cloudy with chalk streaks where I had erased some of my work, and I wondered if a fortune-teller could read eraser marks like tea leaves and, if so, what she would see in my future.

"I think my parents are coming around to college," I said. "We've not talked about it a lot, but when Mrs. Myers made her home visit after Christmas she mentioned it to Mama. And now"—I shrugged—"because I did well . . ."

Mrs. Ballard repeated my words. "And because you did well?"

"I'd like to study math in college," I said, my voice low.

"Ahh, Anna!" Mrs. Ballard turned her head sharply as if I'd almost hit her. "You don't know."

I didn't know what? I knew it was going to take a lot of talking to Daddy about.

"You'll put up with insult and injury. Closed doors and sneers." She took a breath, as if deciding whether to go on. Her eyes were soft and kind, but her words were hard and bitter. "You'll put up with it all, and if you're lucky—and strong enough and good enough— you'll get spit out on the other side like a piece of mauled meat. And"—she made an expansive gesture, including our little room as if it were the Colosseum— "and, you can teach math in the tenth smallest high school in the state. And be expected to be grateful because you have a job. It's a hard road, Anna. And it will end in disappointment."

I was clutching my books so tightly that Meema's bracelet was cutting into my skin. Meema had done what she wanted to do. Maybe she'd chosen to be on the farm with Granddad and raise children. But she'd chosen. I knew she had.

"I think I'm smart enough to do the right thing," I said, my voice shaking.

Mrs. Ballard took a slow breath and let it out. "I don't think you are, Anna."

Then she turned her back to erase the board. There was nothing on it but my old eraser streaks, but she swiped away at it anyway.

I left while she was gathering up her things. I went to the Home Ec room to turn in an assignment to Mrs. Myers. A pink tulip from the senior luncheon had fallen to the floor and somebody had stepped on it, mashing the petals and exposing the smear of crushed yellow insides.

Part 4: Summer

*An equation for me has no meaning
unless it expresses a thought of God.*

—Srinivasa Ramanujan (1887–1920),
self-taught mathematical genius

Chapter 25

$\mathcal{B}$racing the rubber toe of one skate to hold me still, I leaned over the railing of the gazebo. My cheeks were stiff with dried tears of laughter. From this high up, I could see across the park to the concrete building that housed monkeys, a ratty old lion, and a few alligators.

Mike spun to a stop beside me. "How's your finger?" He took my left hand. "Let me see."

My sweaty hand trembled. I had fallen so many times and laughed so hard my body seemed to have no bones.

Mike's T-shirt bloomed with sweat, and his cheeks blazed. He rubbed my little finger. Even though he'd made me immediately stick it in a cup of ice, the tip still had a bruised look from where he'd run over it.

"How many times did I fall?" I asked, taking my hand back and putting it in my pocket. I didn't want to think about losing a nail.

"You're the mathematician," he said. "Can't you work with numbers that big?"

I traced the symbol for infinity, like an eight on its side, on the chipping white paint of the railing. Mike could skate figure eights *and* keep time to the organ music.

Behind us, wheeled feet came down on the floor in a pounding rhythm.

"We have to head home before long," Mike said. "I have to be at work at two."

He'd gotten on the township road crew for the summer, working whenever they needed him.

We turned in our skates, and then drifted over to the little marble basin by the playground that perpetually burbled water. I leaned over it, shutting my eyes against the wad of pink gum somebody had left, and drank until I couldn't hold any more.

We walked past the kiddie pool and tennis courts. At the south end of the park, a small grassy island stuck up in the middle of a shallow lake.

"Let's go over there for a while," I said.

As we crossed the bridge to the island, I looked down at bright little fish tapping against stems of plants.

"When I was a kid, I thought being on a real island was pretty special," I said. "But the water's not even knee deep."

The island had nothing on it except a few park benches and a small wooden platform with a bare trellis used for summer weddings.

We sat down in the shade. My legs tingled from the skating, and the breeze dried my sweat. I took Mike's hand. We watched the ripples in the water and the dragonflies zipping around.

"I'll miss you at school," I said. Summer had just begun, and I already dreaded senior year without Mike.

"I know."

"Do you really want to go in the air force?" Mike was planning to enlist in the fall. "Why don't you do like Mr. Carson and try to work your way through college? We could go together."

"Let me get a jump on college in the air force."

I hated the idea of his going away for four years. "Won't you miss me?"

Mike's eyes flicked to mine. "Do birds fly?"

I wouldn't like Mike trying to talk me out of going to college so I didn't say any more.

"Just remember I love you and everything will be okay," he told me. He freed his fingers from mine and ran them through the short hair on the nape of my neck, spreading his fingers to cup the back of my head.

I leaned back, rocking my head in Mike's hand, looking at the horizon where the tops of the trees touched the pale sky.

After a while, he said, "Tonight?"

I knew what he meant. The desire to meet him at the hickory tree was so gripping that my body almost drifted toward him of its own accord.

I shook my head. "We mustn't."

"Soon?"

Soon it would be a safe time of month for me.

I smiled, touching his face. "Soon. A few more days."

He kissed the palm of my hand.

Chapter 26

When I got home, the twins were barefoot in the yard, trying to hit a badminton birdie back and forth. They waved at Mike. Mama was sitting on the porch watching the girls, a basket of peas beside her and a blue enamel bowl in her lap.

I was supposed to hoe the garden this afternoon, which would take hours. But the rows of tomatoes, peppers, cabbages, and carrots would look so beautiful after I was done that I didn't mind. I preferred my outside chores to helping Mama clean and cook and wash dishes.

The badminton racket pinged as Melanie hit the birdie, and I clapped.

The pea pods made the whole porch smell fresh. "Did you have a good time skating?" Mama asked.

I reached into the basin for a few peas.

"Anna," Mama said, pointing at my wrist.

I wanted to snatch back my hand and put it in my pocket.

Mama took my wrist and turned the clunky ID bracelet so she could read it. "Michael Dillon?"

I'd always worried that someday I might forget to take it off. For a while, I'd been meaning to tell Mama about it anyway. But every time I got to that point, it seemed like something came up: One of the twins needed a Band-Aid or Mama had to settle some squabble between them. And then I didn't want to talk to Mama about my relationship with Mike anymore, and it was easier just to hide the bracelet.

"What's this? Did Mike give this to you today?"

"No, at Christmas." I pulled my hand away.

Why didn't I just say *yes*? Mama would never have known the difference.

"At Christmas?" Surprise widened Mama's eyes. "Well, where has it been all this time?"

I hated this kind of pestering—like exactly what

time the movie would be over or where were Mike and I going.

"Mama, don't worry about it," I said. "I know what I'm doing."

The interest and curiosity in her face turned to anger.

"Could we just not talk about it anymore?" I asked. If I provoked Mama, things would be harder for Mike and me. "I'm sorry I didn't tell you."

But I had awakened the gatekeeper. "Not talk about it!" she said.

"Shhhh, Mama." The badminton birdie landed in the shrub just off the porch, and Cassie came running to get it.

"Girls, go around back and play in the sandbox for a while," Mama commanded.

"But, Mama—" Cassie began.

Mama actually clapped her hands. "Now."

The twins disappeared around the corner, their heads close. Melanie gave us one last glance.

"Anna, what is it we're not going to talk about?" Mama kept after me, but I clenched my teeth together and didn't answer.

She shook her head. "Your daddy and I never meant it to come to this."

"Then you shouldn't have let me go out with Mike in the first place—not when I wasn't even sixteen and you talked Daddy into it."

Mama's face flushed, and I saw her fingers pinching the edge of the bowl in her lap. She stood up and set the bowl on the chair. We were eye to eye.

"Anna, nobody is responsible for your behavior but you."

"That's right, Mama," I said. "So why do we need to talk about it anymore?" I tried to keep my voice light, but Mama could probably tell I wasn't breathing. I *was* responsible for my behavior, and sometimes the fear nearly choked me. Mike and I had made love only twice, but both times I'd cried with relief when my next period came.

"I just thought you and Mike could go out a few times—maybe more as friends and neighbors. But this—" She stopped, seeming to throw up her hands.

"Mama, how can you say that?" It was hypocritical. "You and Daddy have let me go out with Mike any time I wanted to for the last eight months. He goes to church with us! How can you say you didn't know we were more than friends?"

Mama's face showed the truth of what I'd said—

that she and Daddy had looked the other way as long as they could. "Anna—"

She broke off. But then her face hardened. "You're too casual about this, Anna. If you get a bad reputation, it will stay with you forever."

A bad reputation? "Mama, Mike doesn't talk about me," I said, outraged that she'd think such a thing.

"Well, I hope he doesn't have anything to talk *about*, Anna. But if you give in to things, Mike will lose his respect for you." She waited for that to sink in. "And when that happens, you might be surprised what a boy will say."

My eyes stung with tears. How dare she think about Mike and me like that? She made it sound dirty, as though we should be sanitized and pinned on a corkboard and checked on a regular basis. The truth was, she didn't know anything about the way we felt.

"Oh, just go"—I threw up my arms—"just go check on the twins," I said, running into the house, letting the screen door bang behind me.

I waited, holding my breath. Would Mama barge in and tell me I couldn't date Mike anymore?

But the house was totally silent for a long time. I went to my room and shut the door. I sat down at my desk and stared out the window. Mama walked down the drive to the mailbox. I could tell even from the back, by the way she held her head, that I had hurt her.

When she returned from the mailbox, her footsteps sounded in the hallway. She didn't even knock. She just slid the letter under my door.

I was so sidetracked by our blowup that I could hardly understand what the letter said.

Chapter 27

$\mathcal{D}$addy, Mama, and I sat at supper. I brought the letter from its safe place under the edge of the tablecloth into the harshness of the overhead light.

Daddy hadn't come in until dusk, so it was almost nine o'clock. The twins were already in bed.

After grace, Daddy looked at the envelope. "What's that?" he asked with a nod.

I glanced at Mama. Surely she had told him about the letter, about the return address of the New Academy of Mathematics and Sciences. But as my hand lay on the envelope, I knew that neither of them could possibly imagine the miracle of what was inside.

I told them about it. The Academy was gathering

mathematics students at major cities, and I was invited to Chicago on July 19. All expenses for a chaperone and me would be paid.

"How did they get your name?" Daddy asked.

I told him how they'd chosen the first-place, second-place, and third-place winners from all the state math contests. Now they wanted to assemble us for a qualifying exam. Those of us who made the cut would be part of a special advanced studies program while we were still in high school. And, when it was time for college, there might be scholarships.

Daddy reached out his hand for the letter and I gave it to him. I had read the letter so many times that the words unfolded in my own mind right down to the *CC: Milton Carson* as I watched Daddy's eyes move over it.

A veil of sweat cooled my forehead as he went on to page two. The backs of my legs were stuck to the seat of my chair. I raised one and then the other, feeling the sting of damp skin being pried from polished wood.

No matter how I shifted under the beam from the ceiling fixture, I couldn't get comfortable. Mama didn't understand lighting like Meema. The harsh glare seemed to highlight all my faults and sins.

Finally, Daddy passed the letter to Mama.

When she finished reading it and looked up, I began my argument.

First I started with the money part. "It won't cost a single cent," I said. "The letter says all expenses paid."

I looked at Daddy. In my mock debate as I lay on my bed this afternoon waiting for Daddy to come in from the field, his answer had been that there were many things that didn't cost any money, but that didn't mean we did them.

"That's not the point" was what he actually said.

I glanced again at Mama. She was looking at Daddy. Why had I made her so mad at me today?

"But we need to think of the future too," I said. "When the time comes for me to go to college—" I rushed forward, not giving Daddy a chance to demur.

"Your mama and I have already talked about it," Daddy said. "I could put a little land in the soil bank for your college expenses."

I hadn't expected that. I lost the momentum of my argument, and just then the phone rang. Daddy pushed his chair back and went into the living room.

"Yes," he said after a few seconds. "Yes, it came today."

It was Mr. Carson.

Daddy listened. "We are. We're just as proud of Anna as we can be . . . yes . . . yes, it's a great honor."

I squeezed the edges of my chair until I felt like I was denting the wood. I waited, not breathing, hearing the pride in Daddy's voice.

"In spite of all that, Anna's too young," he said. "She's barely sixteen."

I was not barely sixteen. I was sixteen and two months.

"Sure, Milton, you've got Anna's best interests at heart— Yes, I know . . . yes . . . but it would be a wasted trip. Chicago is a long way off. Anna's still too young for all this.

"I know it's important," Daddy said. "But we have to think of Anna. She needs to be with her family. We need to continue raising her the way we see fit. Maybe next year—"

How dare Daddy do this? Next year would be too late.

"Anna." Mama barely breathed my name and I looked at her. "I'm sorry," she said, quietly. She wiped away a tear from her cheek.

I squeezed my own eyes shut, refusing to cry in front of my parents.

I opened them, glaring, when I heard Daddy come back into the room.

"It's not right!" I cried, my voice so thick with tears I couldn't even understand my own words. And I sobbed as I stood up from the table. "I want to go. I want to at least try."

"I'm sorry, honey—" I shrugged away when he tried to touch me as I passed. "Sometimes you just have to trust your parents to know what's best."

By the time I got to my room, I had built up enough rage that Mike probably heard my door slam.

I sat on my bed in the darkness crying until my head pounded.

After a while, Daddy knocked on my door.

"Don't come in," I commanded, my voice thick. "Leave me alone."

He didn't come in, but he didn't leave either. I could see the shadows of his feet in the line of light under the door.

"I'll just talk to you from out here, then," he said. I could hear the strain in his voice. "Your mama and I know you want to go."

He had that only half right. I *was* going.

"You're like Meema in a lot of ways," Daddy said, and I caught my breath in shock.

"Just like her, you've got such a fine talent inside you. It makes your life hard."

I clenched my teeth, not daring to open my mouth for fear of what I might say. How dare he bring up Meema at this moment?

"Meema wanted to study and see the world too," he said. "But if she'd done that, then maybe you wouldn't exist."

I shut my eyes and cried with longing for Meema, and when I looked at the line of light under the door again, Daddy's feet were gone.

All weekend I refused to come out for anything except using the bathroom and silently taking the food that Mama left on a plate in the kitchen. I didn't enter the same room as my parents or speak to anyone, though it hurt my heart to ignore the twins, who stared at me wide-eyed.

Mr. Carson and I would just *go* to Chicago. Our expenses would be paid. I didn't need Daddy to get there. But I knew Mr. Carson would never take it upon himself to do such a thing.

I would go live with Aunt Susie in California. And I'd take the qualifier in San Francisco, the very city Aunt Susie lived in, instead of Chicago. Aunt Susie wasn't an old stick-in-the-mud like Daddy. She'd been an airline stewardess before she got married. She'd seen most of the United States. She'd understand. But I wadded up the letter before I even finished it, not wanting to put Aunt Susie in the position of having to say *no*.

If Meema were here, she'd *make* Daddy do what was right.

I'd stay in my room the rest of my life. I'd never get married. I'd be a crazy old maid and a burden to my daddy. That would show him.

But then I thought about Mike. Twice he'd called, and I'd ignored Mama's announcement that he was on the phone.

Chapter 28

On Saturday, Mike came over.

My face was puffy and I hadn't even brushed my hair, but I still ran outside when I saw the car in the drive.

The car had an odd smell—something very familiar that I couldn't quite name.

"Are you okay?" Mike asked as I slid in the seat beside him.

I told him about the opportunity to go to Chicago. "But Daddy won't let me go. You can't imagine what that trip would mean to me. Just think of the most wonderful thing you ever got to do and multiply it by a million."

"Paint the Sistine Chapel," he said.

I saw on his face the regret for what I was missing.

He took my hand. "I'm sorry," he said. "You would have left them standing in Chicago."

I had to smile at his confidence. "Maybe," I said.

"Can you help me with something?"

"I'll try."

Mike lifted a canvas out of the back and I knew what I'd smelled. The particular combination of turpentine and linseed oil—the smells of Meema's workroom.

"It's my first effort with oil painting," he said, watching my face.

It was a portrait of me.

"It's beautiful," I said.

"Yeah, well . . . I worked from nature."

I felt my face turn red. I certainly didn't look beautiful today. "I mean your work is beautiful."

"I know what you mean," he said, touching my cheek. "Do you think you could help me make a frame?"

"You'd need a miter box."

"All I have is pieces of oak." He pointed to some strips of wood in the back seat.

I knew where we could find a miter box. Meema had one in her workroom. "Let me tell Mama where we're going," I said.

What would Meema's workroom be like after a year? Would Granddad have cleaned it out? Would the miter box still hang on the wall with her other tools?

I directed Mike the way to their house.

The place looked like Granddad was trying. The grass was mowed and Meema's flowerbed was in full bloom.

"I imagine Granddad's out someplace. But he won't mind. I used to live here." I opened the screen door to the kitchen. "Granddad?" One of the porch cats twisted around my ankles in the silence. The quiet house said he wasn't there. I motioned to Mike. "Come in."

Mike gazed around as we walked through the kitchen and dining room to the stairway, his eyes taking in the paintings. "Was your grandmother a professional artist?"

"She probably could have been. In a lot of ways, she just made this house her world. Come on. There should be a miter box upstairs in her workroom."

At the top of the stairs, we turned right. As we came

to my room, I dreaded looking but—at the same time—I wanted to see it. I pushed open the partially closed door.

"This was my room."

We looked at my bed, narrow, with a tall iron headboard twisted into a flower-and-leaf pattern. I had made up that bed almost a year ago, just going through my morning routine, never suspecting that it would be the last time. The quilt was rumpled a little as if somebody had sat on it. Granddad, maybe.

I took Mike's hand and led him inside. The house was so quiet I could almost hear Meema's heart still beating in it.

She had been painting over the mural of fairies and clouds that had been on my bedroom walls as if she knew the change my life would soon be taking. Some of the shapes still showed faintly through the primer, and a half-finished chambered nautilus was emerging in the corner of the north wall. Her yardstick, ruler, and box of charcoal lay on the floor where she'd left them.

I pointed to the center of the spiral of the chambered nautilus. "Meema called this the Eye of God."

Mrs. Ballard would call it the place of infinite density, the approach to zero.

Mike circled his hand on my back, comforting me like I sometimes soothed the twins when they were upset. He hugged me to his side.

I was grateful for the familiar weight of his bracelet on my wrist. I might as well wear it all the time now.

After a while we went into Meema's workroom and got her miter box. She would have been glad to lend it to Mike.

On the way back down the hall, I stepped into my bedroom again, drawing Mike in with me.

"Mike, if it's okay with Granddad, would you finish the mural?"

His eyes widened at the vista of what I was suggesting.

"I know it's not the Sistine Chapel," I said.

He laughed.

I saw the interest in his face as he surveyed the wall.

"I might not have time to finish it—what with working and leaving at the end of the summer."

"I know."

Maybe he didn't really want to do it.

"I'd like to start it though," he told me. "Maybe I could finish it."

"Someday," I said.

He hugged me. "Yeah. Someday."

Monday was the Fourth of July, the first anniversary of Meema's death. I wished I could be with Mike, but he said he had to go to his cousin's house in Mills City. I knew I couldn't spend the day of the Fourth alone in my room.

Chapter 29

The morning of the Fourth, when the twins were outside playing and Daddy was in the field, I left my bedroom door open for the first time since Daddy had said no to Chicago.

This evening we'd be going to the park for fireworks and speeches. Would Granddad go? Our whole lives, we would associate Meema's death with this holiday.

After a while, I looked up to see Mama standing in the doorway. She had a cup of coffee in her hand. "I thought you might like this," she said.

"Thanks."

"May I come in?" Mama asked.

"Yes."

She sat sideways in my desk chair and I sat on the edge of the bed. Our knees almost touched.

"Anna, I'm sorry about the trip to Chicago," she said. "If there was anything I could do, I would."

I felt the tears of the still-fresh wound spark in my eyes.

"You've been hit by two things at once. Not getting to go to Chicago and what today is." She sighed. "And I'm feeling bad because it was really three things at once."

Mama was talking about our argument. About Mike. He was my one comfort. Still, I could tell by Mama's face that she was sorry for the ugliness between us. And I was too.

I didn't trust my voice, so I just shrugged and whispered, "It's okay."

Mama didn't go away, and I cradled the cup in my hands, sipping.

"Since this is the day it is, could we talk a little about Meema?" she asked. "And other things?"

My fingers tensed. I wasn't going to talk about Mike with Mama, but I didn't want to push her away either. "Okay."

"I was only eighteen when I married your daddy," Mama said. "Nineteen when you were born. Although you're just sixteen, sometimes I think you're more mature now than I was when you were born. Actually," she said, her face wobbling between tears and laughter, "I was scared to death of you."

"Scared of me?" A little baby?

"I was. You see, I didn't know what to do. Then the war made everybody's life topsy-turvy. And Meema, who no doubt saw I was terrified, took you into their home, leaving me free to be with my new husband."

I struggled to think of Mama and Daddy like Mike and me—not sure about what was the right thing to do. Maybe Daddy had been scared too, about the war and being away from home.

"And when things finally settled down," Mama said, "you had become Meema and Granddad's child. And nobody could blame you. Nobody could blame Meema either, though I did for a while."

Now I finally understood what had caused the distance between Mama and Meema.

"When you were twelve, the twins came along, and I was an old lady of thirty by then." Mama smiled. "And I knew what it meant to really be a mother."

I'd always seen the closeness, the magnetism, be-tween Mama and the twins, something I'd never had.

"And that's when I was grown-up enough to be down-on-my-knees grateful that you had that bond with Meema. At least you *had* it." Tears were rolling down Mama's face. "And who would ever have imag-ined that Meema would die when you were right at the point in your life of needing her most."

I pulled my knees up, hugging them, my face turned away from Mama. I didn't want her to see my pain. It was like my feelings for Mike. Too private.

Mama just sat there. But I couldn't think of any-thing to say. I didn't blame her. It wasn't her fault. It just *was*.

I jumped at the sudden touch of her hand on my head. She stroked my hair, and I let hot tears run across my face and down my bare legs. After a while, the tears tickled so much that I couldn't stand it. I sat up and reached for the tissue Mama handed me.

"Maybe what you need now," Mama said, blowing her own nose, "is a combination mother and friend." There was a look on her face as if she knew the worst was over. "And I'm volunteering."

I wiped my face and nodded.

"Okay then," she said, standing up. She held out her arms. As we hugged and rocked, she circled her hand on my back, then held me away. "I've got to man the booth at the park for the Ladies Aid this afternoon. Would you like to go with me? The twins could stay here, and later everybody could ride in with Granddad for the fireworks."

Mama and I had hardly ever spent any time alone together, without the twins. Without Meema.

Chapter 30

$\mathcal{I}$ stood with Mama at the Ladies Aid stand, helping raffle off the coconut cakes and monkey bread and pecan pies that the members had donated. Finally, as dusk was settling, I drifted over to the bandstand.

At the band shell, the Baxter Municipal Band played Sousa marches. And right before the fireworks, a real United States senator was supposed to make a speech.

I wished Carolyn could be here for the celebration, but she'd gone to Wisconsin to babysit a little cousin whose mother worked. The regular babysitter was having surgery. So for six whole weeks, Carolyn would make twenty-five cents an hour, eight hours a day, five days a week. She would come home rich.

Daddy, Granddad, and the twins came through the crowd. The twins held balloons twisted into the shapes of dogs.

"Find us seats," Daddy said, turning the twins over to me. "I'll get your mother. The speech will be starting soon."

"And then the fireworks!" Cassie said.

"Anna!"

I turned to see Mr. Carson. "Anna!" he said. "And your family. Hello, sir." He stuck out his hand to Daddy and then Granddad.

We stood, everybody smiling at everybody until Daddy said, "The seats are about all gone."

"There's room here," Mr. Carson said, "if you'd like to sit with me."

Just then somebody came on stage holding a microphone and asked us to stand for the singing of "The Star-Spangled Banner." The band played and a pretty girl with a strong voice led the singing. Mama found us in the crowd.

She sat at the end between Daddy and Mr. Carson. The man with the microphone introduced William T. Bailey, our United States senator, and talked about how honored the town was to have such a distinguished person with us.

Senator Bailey wasn't a very big man, but his voice sounded full over the public address system. He said what a grand country America was and how it had fought for its independence. "Now," he said, looking out over the audience, "we have to fight a different kind of war against Communist Russia."

He talked about the country's preparations to win this new war. About the space program. About education programs.

I watched pale stars blossom in the twilight. The Russians had launched satellites that circled the earth. Maybe I was seeing one right now.

"Our government is committing millions of dollars to catching up with the Russians," the senator was saying. "Some of those dollars are going directly into the space program, but many are going into education. Money is being poured into high school and college mathematics and science programs. We're investing in our young people because we know our schools must graduate the best students in the world to guarantee our future as a free country."

Mr. Carson nudged me. When I looked at him, he nodded toward Daddy.

Was Daddy listening? Was he thinking that what the senator was saying might possibly apply to the New Academy of Mathematics and Sciences? And me?

Senator Bailey went on to talk about appropriations and budgets and national security.

I watched Daddy's face.

The senator ended his remarks as the sky darkened enough for the fireworks.

The first wave of booming color frightened the twins, who buried their faces in Mama's lap.

As the fireworks continued to burst and flare over the treetops, layers of smoke hung in the air and drifted in a cloud over the park. Finally, on cue, the band broke into "God Bless America" and the fireworks people on the island let loose with a huge, booming bouquet of pyrotechnics.

As we were gathering up our things, Mr. Carson said to Daddy, "Anna's the kind of person that senator was referring to. That's what all the money is for. It's for programs like the New Academy of Mathematics and Sciences. And for gifted young people like Anna. It's a shame to waste that money, sir."

Daddy hated wasting money more than snakes.

I wanted to hug Mr. Carson because he never gave up.

He pressed on. "They wouldn't have offered to pay two people's way to Chicago if they didn't know Anna was a good investment."

I held my breath in an unutterable prayer.

"She's very mature for her age."

"She is," Mama said, putting her arms around my shoulders.

Daddy seemed to be surveying the area for any possessions we might have left, but I saw his expression begin to change.

Finally, he looked at Mr. Carson. "Do you suppose it's too late?"

"I'm sure it's not," Mr. Carson said.

I shivered in the warm night and looked at the stars.

Oh brave new world!

"Thank you," I whispered.

Chapter 31

As we rode north to Chicago, I went to the dining car with Daddy and nearly fainted when a waiter flapped open a large white linen napkin and laid it in my lap.

When we finally got off the train after six hours, Daddy hailed a cab and we alternately bolted and crept through the traffic. The taxi driver had the windows down, and the metallic smell of the hot pavement and exhaust rolled through the cab.

At the hotel, we were given a room on the twelfth floor, higher than I had ever been in my life. My stomach did a little dance as the uniformed attendant stopped the elevator and announced, "Twelfth floor. Watch your step," and opened the doors.

We ate in the hotel coffee shop, and Daddy told me stories of the places he and Mama had traveled to during World War II when I was with Granddad and Meema.

I spotted several other people my age in the room—probably here for the same reason I was. One of the boys smiled at me.

The next morning, as we were finding seats in an auditorium on the University of Chicago campus, I saw the same boy again. This time he looked at me oddly.

A man stepped to the podium and we gave him instant silence.

"Welcome," he said. "Thank you for coming. As you know from the material you've been getting in the mail, the reason you're here is because we know you're very bright young people. One arm of the New Academy of Mathematics and Sciences has been funded specifically to identify you and give you a head start. For some of you, this will mean scholarships at the best universities. For others, it will mean an opportunity to study mathematics on a more advanced level than your high school can probably offer you at present."

The man finished by explaining how we'd draw tickets out of a box as we left the auditorium. Each ticket had one of ten room numbers written on it. Each room was assigned five students. Our teams would be randomly determined according to which ticket we picked.

I flowed with the crowd toward the door, drawing a ticket with the number 214 on it. It wasn't a perfect number. It wasn't even a prime. "Down that way, second door on the right," somebody said, glancing at my ticket and pointing.

At the door to room 214, Daddy gave my arm a quick squeeze, and in only seconds, four boys were in the room with me and someone at the door said, "Any supplies you might need are on the bookshelf. You have until two o'clock. Good luck!"

I caught a glimpse of Daddy as the door closed. How had it all happened so fast? I was here.

Chapter 32

$\mathcal{F}$ive chairs circled the round table. A single sheet of paper had been placed at each spot. A stack of blue books lay in the middle.

"This is it?" The boy who asked that had an accent like Mike's dad.

"This is it!" another boy said. He had an accent too. "George Andersen. Milwaukee."

"I'm Anna Conway. My daddy and I took the train up yesterday."

George smiled. "Up from a long way down?"

From their point of view, I was the one who talked funny. I felt a jab of loneliness for Bud, who spoke exactly like me.

"I'm Dale Schmidt," the one with the Chicago accent said. "My dad's a professor here."

The boy with the frizzy hair inventorying the bookshelf was Nick, and the one looking out the window was Chris.

Then the room went as silent as if we were waiting for somebody to say grace before a meal. I touched Meema's charm bracelet, and its faint jingling drew their eyes.

A thin red hand swept away the seconds on the wall clock. It had begun.

I sat down and picked up the sheet of paper. First word—*Prove* . . .

The muscles in my back knotted, making me sit up straighter. Most of what I knew about proofs had come from Mrs. Ballard.

We were asked to prove any one of five statements using Euclid's first four axioms. The axioms were at the bottom of the page.

"They even gave us the axioms," Dale mused.

I returned to the top of the page. The first statement to be proved was a parallel lines statement: *Two parallel lines are equidistant.* There was nothing very complicated about that. I felt my muscles relax. I rested my arms on the table and read the second statement, also about parallel lines.

"Do these look simple to you guys?" George said, peering at his paper as if the real problems were written in invisible ink. "What's the deal?"

I read the remaining statements. They had to do with parallel lines also and looked almost equally straightforward.

"I guess we could each take one and prove it," Nick suggested, patting his hair.

"Nah," Chris said, "let's work together. We're supposed to be a team, right? That's why they put us in the same room."

"I agree," Dale said. "They probably want us to demonstrate teamwork."

It was okay with me. I felt dizzy with wonder.

"Okay. We need somebody at the board," Dale announced. "A recorder."

Everybody looked around the circle, their eyes all stopping at the same place. Recorder—secretary—girl. Carolyn was right. Girls had to know how to take dictation. But what difference did it make now? I was here.

I walked to the front of the room.

Chapter 33

"The first statement is to show that two parallel lines are equidistant," George said, reading from the sheet.

I drew two horizontal lines as arrows pointing forever in both directions. I labeled the top one L and the bottom one M. To one side, I wrote *GIVEN: L is parallel to M*. Below that, I wrote *TO PROVE: L and M are equidistant*.

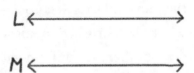

It was easy to see what came next.

"If we're going to measure the distance between the lines, we should drop some perpendiculars from L to M. Make a rectangle," Nick suggested.

I was already reaching to draw the perpendiculars, but paused when he said *rectangle*. Mrs. Ballard would call that begging the question. Should I say something? I didn't want to, but I hoped someone would.

Dale rescued us. "We don't know that it's a rectangle," he said. "If we knew that, we'd know the parallel lines are equidistant. Because AC and BD would have to be congruent."

"You can't assume what you have to prove," George chimed in.

I drew the verticals. Then I marked the right angles and labeled the vertices A, B, C, and D.

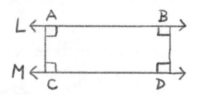

"It *looks* like a rectangle," I admitted, for Nick's sake.

We threw ourselves into the effort of proving it.

We had no shortage of ideas and, for a while, it was fun. But as time passed, so did our smiles. We couldn't prove the figure a rectangle.

We tried other ways of proving the parallel lines equidistant. I drew a diagonal from A to D and we tried to show that the right triangles that resulted would be congruent, so their corresponding sides would be congruent. I was certain that was the way to show AC and BD marked the same distance, but we couldn't do it. We tried shuffling the right angles and still made no progress.

Chris sat on the window ledge playing with the cord of the blind. In growing frustration over the would-be rectangle, Nick was twirling his hair into corkscrews. Sweat made the waistline of my blouse damp.

How had almost an hour passed? Could that be right?

"Look, we don't have to prove every statement," Chris reminded us from the window. He spun the end of the cord so fast it hummed.

"Yeah," George said, ceasing his doodling, "let's just go on. The next one will be easier."

The statement that we had just spent an hour on had initially looked pretty easy too.

"And waste all the time we've invested in this

one?" Nick wailed. "Come on, guys. I'll bet we're almost there. And I've got an idea."

Nick wanted to draw two diagonals and show that two of the isosceles triangles formed were congruent. It was a good idea and gave us another dose of hope, but we were left even more discouraged when we couldn't do it. More and more it seemed we'd been given an impossible task.

My nose itched with chalk dust and nerves. And at the window, Chris had fallen silent, intent on fashioning the cord into a hangman's noose.

"Remember the principles of test taking," Dale coached. "Don't get bogged down on one problem. Especially not in this case, where we don't even have to prove every statement."

"Yeah. Okay," Nick finally agreed. "We'll leave it. Let's move on."

I tried to slow my heart, to hold back panic. It had looked so *easy* to begin with.

Mrs. Ballard had warned me.

Lunch came when we had given up on the proofs for the second and third statements and had begun a so-far-unsuccessful attack on the fourth one.

"This is ridiculous," George exclaimed, banging the pencil he'd been incessantly doodling with on the table so hard the lead broke. "Rectangles. Triangles. Congruency. None of that is in the axioms. What are we doing using them?"

The question went unanswered.

I gazed at the tray of sandwiches. How could anybody eat?

"Gotta get our energy up," Nick said, grabbing a sandwich.

"Keep working," Dale urged. His shirt had come untucked on one side and curves of wetness lined the underarms.

George was right. The four axioms we were given were just the fundamental statements about points and lines. They didn't give us anything about rectangles or triangles or . . . or *parallel lines*.

It was like being banged in the face—so shocking that I didn't feel the pain for a minute. And then I did.

I shambled to the board. "Look at this." I drew two nearly horizontal lines that sloped slightly toward each other, then a vertical line through both of them.

When I marked the angles, Dale smacked the heel of his hand against his forehead, and I knew he recognized what I'd drawn.

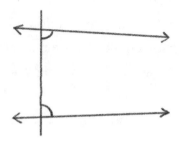

"Euclid's fifth axiom," he said. "His parallel line axiom. If those angles add up to less than 180 degrees, then the lines will intersect. But if they sum 180, then the lines are parallel."

The room grew still.

I wiped my palms on my skirt, remembering what Mrs. Ballard had told us about the history of Euclid's fifth axiom—namely that Euclid himself had wondered whether it was really an independent axiom. Could it be proved from the first four? Or did it have to stand on its own?

I remembered how Mrs. Ballard put it. *The work of later mathematicians showed that Euclid's parallel line postulate had to be an independent axiom because the other axioms couldn't support it.* So how could we expect them to support our parallel line statements?

"I'm pretty sure you can't prove parallel line statements with Euclid's first four axioms," I said, laying down the nub of chalk that seemed to weigh fifty pounds. "At least, not according to my geometry teacher."

They sat and stared at me, too beaten down to react.

After a while, Chris just shook his head. "I believe it." He twisted a piece of paper into an effigy, slipped the hangman's noose over its head, and let it swing.

We were dead.

"So now we're saying that it's impossible? They gave us an impossible test?" George's voice rose. He put his broken pencil between his teeth and crunched down.

I shivered at the sound.

"I hope it is impossible. That way failure's not our fault," Nick said.

"Anna, do you by any chance know the *proof* that these statements can't be proven from the axioms?" Dale asked.

"No."

"So what should we do?" Nick's question circled and settled, unanswered.

"We have to get something on paper," Dale said. "And quoting Anna's math teacher probably isn't going to cut it. We should show our efforts even if they haven't led to a proof."

"I just wish we knew what we're dealing with here," George ranted, throwing his pencil straight up into the air. "What's the point of giving us an impossible task?"

My feet stung, my neck ached.

"Maybe they just want to see how well we hold up under pressure," Nick mused.

I longed to wash the chalk dust off my hands.

"Maybe they're considering how we work as a team." Dale shrugged. "At least we didn't kill each other."

Nick swung the hanged man.

We hadn't done well.

I had to get out of the room.

In the bathroom, I bent over the sink, splashing my face, and then let tepid water run on my wrists, feeling like I might have to run into the stall and throw up.

What was Daddy doing? Was he thinking two o'clock was never going to get here?

Well, it wouldn't be much longer. I'd go home and shut up about studying mathematics.

I let the water run higher, trickling over Meema's and Mike's bracelets. Then I turned off the faucets and stared into the mirror.

Mirrors reversed images.

That's why Meema used to hold her paintings to the mirror or turn them upside down to check their compositions.

Turn them upside down. That's the phrase Mrs. Ballard used when she explained *reductio ad absurdum.*

Negating the statements might pay off, she said. Turn a statement upside down, she said, and money might fall out of its pockets. If the opposite of what you were trying to prove was absurd—if it contradicted what was true—then the original statement had to be true.

I pictured the five parallel line statements in my mind. One by one, I rolled their logic upside down and gazed at their ridiculous new state.

And it wasn't necessarily absurd. There was no contradiction with the first four axioms. That was the mystery and the miracle. *It wasn't absurd.*

I held that idea in perfect, timeless calm for an instant, and then I remembered the boys and the clock and all that hinged on writing something intelligent in the blue book. We were almost out of time, but I had to hold on to my insight. I was sure I'd fall over and die if I had grasped something this important and returned empty-handed.

I raced back to the room.

The boys looked up from the table.

"What?" Nick said.

"I have an idea. If we have time"—I gestured to the clock. *If I could express it*—"we need to turn the statements on their heads."

Disappointment reshaped Dale's face. "*Reductio ad absurdum*. We were just talking about that."

"For Pete's sake," Chris grumbled, "that won't win us any prizes."

"But we could write it down," George said, giving me my hook. "At least we'll have *something*. At least we can show them we recognize the contradiction."

"Wrong," I said, full of so much energy I could have run through the streets of Chicago yelling *Eureka!* "That's wrong. We *don't* recognize the contradiction."

I had their attention.

Finally Chris spoke in the silence. "We don't?"

"We don't recognize that any of the opposites of those five statements are contradictions," I said.

I flew back to the board, dancing chalk across the surface. I sliced a horizontal line and swooped a curved line above it, making a big smile. "These two parallel lines are *not* equidistant," I declared.

I didn't give them time to object. I started drawing the opposite of statement two.

"Wait, wait, wait," Chris was saying.

But I didn't stop until I'd drawn two lines parallel to the same line but not parallel to each other.

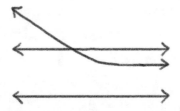

I was moving on to the next statement when Chris yelled, "Stop already!"

"What?" I demanded. "I'm drawing the opposites."

"But you're curving the lines."

I took a deep breath and prepared for the final push to the edge.

"It looks crazy, Anna," Nick said.

"That's what contradictions look like," George muttered, starting to copy my work onto paper.

"Listen," I said, holding my hands up like a traffic policeman. "George. Repeat after me. *They aren't contradictions.*"

"So what are they, then?" Dale frowned, but he was doing his best to stay on the trail. "If they aren't contradictions, we don't even have any last-ditch *reductio ad absurdum* proofs."

"They're counterexamples," I said, and closed my eyes, waiting for the uproar that would follow.

Counterexamples without contradictions.

But I heard only silence.

"Counterexamples?" Chris finally said. "But they can't be counterexamples. You've curved the lines."

I opened my eyes. As certain as I felt, my fingers were shaking as I drew the chalk downward along the board, leaving a vertical line that I capped at both ends with arrows that pointed on forever. I drew a line across it and then another. The sum of the interior angles was less than 180 degrees. The last line was bound to intersect the second—*until* I curved it, sending it into a spiral.

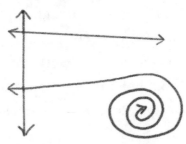

"There!" Chris called out. "That's the problem. You can't curve the lines like that. These statements all talk about *straight* lines."

I looked at Dale, thinking he might be the most likely to follow where I was trying to lead. But it was Nick who said, "She's right. The axioms say a line can go on forever and can be drawn between two points. The axioms don't say that a straight line can't curve."

"They say straight lines can be extended, but they don't control where they go. They say straight lines can go from point to point, but they don't dictate how they get there," I said, drawing crazy lines all over the board.

"We got about three minutes left, guys," Dale said.

"Make sure we get it down. Maybe Anna has found the loophole."

I watched Chris's expression as he struggled with *curved* straight lines. It was like I was asking him to find the square root of negative one. I wondered if Descartes would call these *imaginary* straight lines.

Our statement in the blue book was a single sentence. *The included diagrams show each of the statements is unsupported by the given axioms.* We decided to hand in my drawing of Euclid's fifth too. Extra credit!

As we sat, waiting for the door to open, I thought about Mrs. Ballard. I was glad I listened to her. But not about everything. Disproving her was good too.

Chapter 34

"Thank you," a man said, taking the booklet. He glanced at the thickness of eraser marks on the board, walked over to the window, and freed the hanged man. He studied it.

"Anybody I'd recognize?" he asked, handing it to Chris.

How had he known it was Chris who had hanged the man?

Chris blushed and wadded up the effigy. "No, sir," he said.

As we left, I saw Nick glance into the mirror over the bookshelf, smooth his hair, then lean closer.

Outside in the hall, students, chaperones, and staff

funneled toward the main hallway. I spotted Daddy and waved.

Dale tucked in his shirttail, trying to go back to looking intelligent instead of a little bit crazy. "My dad's waiting for me in his office," he said.

"Good luck," I told him. "I really hope you make it. I think you will."

He shrugged, smiling. "Good luck to all of us." And he turned away.

"There's your bus, folks," a staff member said. "It will take you to the hotel."

On the bus, Nick, George, Chris, and I went to the back. I leaned my head against a half-open window, trying to see the tops of the tall buildings.

"How did that guy know it was Chris who'd done the hangman?" George asked, turning to talk over the back of the seat where he and Nick were sitting.

"One out of five," Chris said. "It could have been luck."

"One out of four," I corrected him. "Girls don't hang people. We cut them up with fingernail scissors."

"It could have been a two-way mirror," Nick said.

"What's that?" I asked.

"Don't you ever watch TV?"

"We don't have one."

"Well, see"—Nick leaned near me—"remember the mirror over the bookshelf? Which seems kind of weird now that I think of it. That mirror could have been for observation. For people to watch us. Watch what we did. What we put on the board. Watch Chris hang the man."

He jabbed Chris and Chris groaned.

"That's creepy." I shivered at the idea of strangers seeing what had happened in that room. But it was exciting too. Had Daddy been able to watch?

Later, when the train was rocking and clacking south, I asked him. "Could you see us, Daddy? Some of the boys on the team decided maybe we were being observed. Were we?"

He nodded. "They had a real clever layout. You all were in ten rooms. Five on each side around this long, narrow room where we waited. There was a window where we could look into each room."

"So did all the teams have the same problem?" I asked. "Did we all have to do the same thing?"

"I'm pretty sure you did. I couldn't follow most of it. But at the end, when you were talking about turning things upside down and counterexamples, everybody was ganged up around your window."

"What did they say?"

He laughed. "One of them said, 'That little lady just curved space!'"

"What else?"

"Something about a higher geometry."

Chapter 35

The acceptance letter came the next week, and Daddy read parts of it over and over to Mama, Granddad, the twins, and even Mike. Except for the sin of pride, he probably would have sent it to the newspaper.

Personally, the part I liked best was the second paragraph.

> Miss Conway, you demonstrated a
> sound knowledge of mathematics,
> which speaks highly of your
> teachers. You were a team player,
> often assuming a leadership role.

But most of all, the committee was impressed by the imagination and creativity that you brought to the table.

I know Daddy liked that part too, because he kept talking about how the New Academy people had been huddled around our window as I allegedly "curved space." But I'm pretty sure his *absolute* favorite part was the paragraph about scholarship money.

Mrs. Ballard heard about the Chicago trip too, probably through Mr. Carson. And she called one day, wanting me to tell her all about it. I enjoyed being able to discuss the problem with someone who really understood what our team had done. As I talked, she made little exclamations of despair and delight. Finally, at the end, when I described the crazy spirals and swoops of my straight lines, she laughed. "Next year, I'll tell you about Gauss and Riemann," she said.

I had no idea what she meant, but I looked forward to it.

Mama suggested a party to celebrate. Plus, Granddad's birthday was coming up.

"Have the party here," Granddad offered. "This

house needs a party in it." His voice broke. "Meema would be so proud of you, Anna." His face twisted, and he put his hand over his mouth.

"I know," I said, slipping my arm around him.

The next week, Mama and I baked and cooked in Meema's kitchen. One afternoon while I was waiting for lemon bars to come out of the oven, I went up to my old room and stretched out on the bed. I listened to Mama working in the kitchen, washing dishes and putting things in the cupboard.

The upstairs smelled faintly of turpentine again, just as it had when Meema was alive. Mike had worked on the chambered nautilus and painted in the textured bark of a hickory tree.

I rested awhile and then I went to the head of the stairs and called Mama to come up.

"I've not been in this room for years." She stood in the doorway. "I'll bet you were cozy here."

I nodded.

"It looks like Mike has taken over the project," she mused, studying the wall. "I wonder what it would have been like if Meema had been able to finish it for you?"

I wondered too. Some of our plans unfolded just as we planned, and others didn't.

"Meema had great imagination," Mama said. "So does Mike."

That's what the letter from the New Academy had said about me. That I had imagination.

The Saturday night of the party, we opened the house to the smell of the hay Granddad had cut that afternoon. And the petunias let loose their sweetness outside the sunroom windows.

Granddad's neighbors and people from the church gathered in the living room and dining room and sunroom. Mike and his parents were there. And Carolyn and Bud. And Mr. Carson and Mrs. Ballard.

After everybody gathered around the table to sing "Happy Birthday" to Granddad, Mr. Carson launched himself into "You Are My Sunshine," beaming at me.

Behind Mr. Carson's back, Carolyn rolled her eyes a little, but I thought he had a nice voice.

Mike stood beside me as Mr. Carson sang.

Everyone joined in and, when he finished, everybody clapped for everybody else and Granddad blew out his candles, which had melted and scorched some of the icing.

Later, when we were home, Mike pushed me in the swing. Probably I was getting too old for such things, but I liked the wind lifting my hair off my face and cooling my legs. Last night, I had lain curled against Mike's side when I asked him why he loved me. The moon was just bright enough to show his expression. He was smiling. "I don't know," he said. "But I do."

"Anna, you'll get chiggers," Daddy announced from the porch. "You too, Mike."

"I want to swing awhile longer, Daddy, okay?" I called toward the darkness of the front porch. "And then I'll be in. We won't be long."

Silence.

But finally he spoke. "Okay. Just a little longer. Then you go on home, Mike."

"Yes, sir."

I pumped, stretching my bare feet toward the stars, seeming to pause on the edge of something grand, then sailing backward. Over and over, making my own breeze, hearing the air move past my ears and the tree frogs singing.

Finally, I leapt out, flying through the air.